DETOURS

DEAD ENDS

by Aurelio Rico Lopez III

HellBound Books Publishing LLC

**A HellBound Books LLC
Publication**

www.hellboundbookspublishing.com

Printed in the United States of America

DETOURS

DEAD ENDS

A HellBound Books Publishing LLC Book
Houston TX

Salute mi familia.

Contents

DETOURS

DEAD ENDS

SKIN DEEP

It's an impulse,
A dreadful compulsion –
One I cannot rightly ignore
That I base opinion
Solely on appearance.
I understand beauty –
Or lack thereof –
Is merely skin deep,
That I am to see past
One's physique before
Condemning him
And passing judgment.
Yet, I gaze into those dark eyes
And the fat, forked tongue
Dangling, eel-like from
Severed, horned head
And realize I do not
Have the luxury of
Getting to know a demon.

PLAY TIME

Sunlight glitters
Off the water surface
As the waves roll onto shore.
Each of Poseidon's saline curls
Reaches its destination.
Rhythm peaceful, relaxing.
A Beach Boys tune plays
From speakers in the distance,
A pleasant background
To the laughter and
Whoops of joy of the afternoon crowd.
An explosion of saltwater,
A shrill cry of horror.
The sea churns red.
Cheer turns to chaos.
Swimmers paddle for shore;
Many of those who make it
Are trampled to death
By the terrified crowd.
As horrid as their deaths are,
They are a blessing
Compared to what's to come.

Tentacles burst out of the sea
As tall as skyscrapers.
Appendages crash to the ground
Plucking three, four people at a time.
It is over in five minutes,
Just as the next Beach Boys song
Comes to an end.

THE NIGHT BEFORE

The shadow creeps through the house,
Unseen and unheard.
Fireplace warms the home,
Though, in history, similar flames
Had burnt witches and
Outcasts at the stake.
The air smells of gingerbread cookies,
With an acrid hint of cigarette smoke,
And stockings hang bloated like
Giant, gravid slugs about to pop.
Intruder ascends the staircase,
Moving with surprising agility
For such a heavy man.
He heads toward the bedrooms
And stops in front of the door
Featuring a pirate ship and
A sign that says:
Intruders will walk the plank.
He smiles and pulls out a gift –
A small, yet heavy box,
Wrapped in silver paper and
Tied in a golden bow.

He sets the present just inside
Of the young boy's door.
Normally, he would leave it under
The tree, among the other presents,
But he wants it to be the
First thing Paul sees in the morning.
A gift for a fine, brave pirate
Who had lost his mother
A little over a year ago.
The stranger's smile vanishes as
He glances over to the door that
Leads to the bedroom of boy's stepdad.
He reins his emotions and returns
Downstairs.
He remembers the heartbreaking letter
The boy sent him,
 and learning
About the shocking things he had
To endure under the custody
Of his legal guardian every night.
By principle, the crimson-dressed stranger
Could not take matters into his hands,
But that didn't mean he couldn't help.
This season was for the kids, after all.
He just hoped the young pirate
Would figure out how to work the safety.

CEREMONY

The sun is a dearly departed relative
Gently lowered
Into its horizon grave.
Splotches of orange, red, and blue
Blot the sky.
The heavens weep,
Casting droplets like
A thousand condolences
In attempt to assuage grief.
The wind whispers
A mournful hymn of loss
As stars appear one by one
To pay their respect,
And night shamelessly saunters
Without invitation
Or provocation,
A greedy mistress
Intent on raising hell.

FIRST DRAFT

He purses his lips;
Brows furrowed in concentration.
Has to get message across.
The message is key,
Otherwise, what's the point?
Might as well
Pack up and go home.
More and more,
His followers grow.
Thank God for social media.
But he knows fame is fleeting,
Transient;
You are only as good
As your last work.
No pressure.
Yeah, right.
He steps back to admire his work,
Sheaths the knife,
Wipes his blood-stained hands
With a dirty rag, and wonders
Will the critics get it?

INVISIBLE

I trip and get up,
Hand pressed against my side.
Blood seeps through
My fingers, ignoring
My pathetic attempt
To staunch the wound.
Muscles burn as if
They were doused in kerosene
And set ablaze.
Empty alley;
I lean against the side
Of the building for support,
Vision clouding.
I sense movement behind me,
And I know he's coming
To finish the job.
Fight or flight.
The fight is out of me,
So flight it is.
I stumble through empty cartons
And a puddle of piss,
Accidentally kicking a tin can and

Scaring a pair of rats.
They squeak in anger,
But I have more pressing matters
To deal with.
My assailant draws closer
And I picture the knife in his hand.
Up ahead, on the sidewalk,
A man wearing dark glasses
Turns to me.
I wave frantically to catch his attention.
If I can get him to help
Or call the police–
As the blade buries itself
Deep into my throat,
The last image I see is the
Walking stick
In the witness's right hand.

BALANCE

Under the sickly glow of
A lantern resting on top of
A pale gray headstone,
The shovel cuts through the soil
As a medical examiner's scalpel
Would a deceased body.
The cemetery, filled with its
Hundreds of silent residents,
Remains hushed
Except for the occasional
Grunt of exertion and
The cadence of the shovel blade
Defiling the earth.
The stranger pauses,
Wipes his brow, and glances
Casually at the trunk
Of his sedan parked nearby.
Some would say removing
A dead body from the grounds
Was a macabre form of theft,
But it wasn't so much stealing
As it was replacing.

GAMER

Enchantresses and orcs,
Wolves, demons, and zombies...
Yours is a fight for survival.
Ordeals of courage, grit, and
Cunning.
An entire world
For the price of a few dollars,
Each level harder than
The one before.
You forge on
With swords, shotguns,
Spells, crowbars, machetes,
Bare hands, and cunning.
This is who you are, who
You were meant to be.
Not the loser whose
Boss forces him
To work overtime,
Not the pariah trapped in
A 4 x 4 foot cubicle,
Prisoner to a dead-end job.

You are the hero,
Slayer of monsters,
Saviour of kingdoms!
Now gut this bitch, and
Claim your prize.

BONE DRY

(THAT MIGHT NOT

HAVE BEEN A LIZARD)

The driver eyes me through
The rear view mirror
Before refocusing his attention
On the road.
I glance out the rear side window.
All I see is dust and rock
And the occasional desert shrub,
Fighting for survival.
Bone dry.
For the moment,
I am thankful the vehicle has
Air-conditioning.
One of the wonders of science;
You'd be sweating out
A Biblical flood outside,
But inside, you're at risk of
Testicular frostbite.
I see movement by the side
Of the road;
It may have been a lizard –
One of those ugly fucks
With horns.
Then again, I may have
Imagined it.

I stare down at my lap,
At my hands bound by duct tape,
And I know this part of the story
Isn't imagination,
Neither is the fat bastard
Beside me,
Pressing the barrel of the
.45 calibre pistol against
The side of my ribcage.
Outside, the sun bakes the land.
Bone dry.
You could lose things out there;
You could lose things,
And no one would ever know.

FILL 'ER UP

He taps the brakes and eases
The sedan into the gasoline station,
Pulls up to the pumps
And kills the engine.
Headlights off.
Ahead, the road vanishes –
A fleeting vision,
Like a dream eluding recollection
Upon the dreamer's awakening.

Driver steps out of the vehicle.
Just a quick stop.
He enters the store and
Approaches the cashier.
How's it going?
Just need to fill up the tank.
Haven't I seen you before?
I doubt that very much.
Say, aren't you that guy on TV?

A moment of silence,
Then, a gunshot,

Loud and final.
Seconds later, the man steps out of the shop,
Climbs back into the car.
His sigh is heavy with grief.
The engine rumbles back to life;
Dream resumes once more as he drives
Toward the next station.

ALONE IN THE YARD, A LOADED GUN IN ONE HAND

It is night.
He stands in the middle of the yard,
Still, like a scarecrow
With a loaded gun in one hand,
A half-empty bottle
Of whiskey in the other.
The sickening scent of jasmine
Tickles his nostrils.
He remembers planting them
In the garden a year and a half ago.
Dreams feeding off deception
And lies,
Blooming infidelity.
The air is cold but anger
Keeps him warm.
His grip tightens around the
Revolver.
His best friend's car parked in
Front of the house.

They thought he'd be back tomorrow.
Anger takes another swig
Of whiskey.
Time to say hello to the wife.

MONSTROUS

It rests in the corner
Of the dusty room,
Hidden behind drapes of
Shadow.
Teddy lies on the floor.
Left leg missing,
White, fluffy innards
Pouring forth
From eviscerated belly.
The room holds its breath
In trepidation,
Cautious not to wake
The slumbering babe.
Outside, clouds tread
Carefully across the
Night sky.
Old floorboard creaks,
And glowing eyes
Snap open.
Small, gray hand grips
Edge of crib,
And an impatient wail

Echoes throughout
The house.
Lips peel back in
A hideous snarl
As the creature demands
To be fed once more.

THE THING

There was a thing
That was not meant to be,
But intended or not,
It existed.
Grown in a laboratory,
The thing was unaware
Of its existence and
Knew not of its creators
Or their intentions.
It spent its time –
Though it had no concept
Of seconds, minutes, days,
Or weeks –
In a petri dish,
But there was no satisfaction
Or discontent for its
Living arrangement.
One evening,
A young scientist,
Exhausted from hours of work,
Knocked over the dish.
He panicked as he inhaled,

Screamed as the flesh
Melted off his face and arms.
And the thing felt
Neither joy nor remorse
As it found its way
To the air vents.
It was what it was,
Intended or not.

SYMPHONY

Eyes closed,
Concentration imperative.
Focus.
Years of practice
Have led to this day –
His opus.
This is the one
He will be remembered for;
Of that, he is certain.
The conductor struggles
To steady his breathing,
Slow his pulse.
He allows the moment
To take hold,
Gives in to the flow.
She unleashes a blood-curdling
Scream before gasping
Her final breath.
Eyes closed.
Music to his ears.

HAIL TO THE KING

Forked tongue spews lies;
It is a different language entirely.
Yet the masses gather by the
Tens of thousands
To listen to the messiah's words.
One after the other,
Blatant promises are made,
False covenants that play
With one's weaknesses,
Insecurities, and desires.
He vomits death and oppression,
And they sing him songs of praise.
He is their golden calf,
The reincarnation of an ancient god;
He is the saviour,
The right hand of justice.
He is the sword dangling
By a string,
Perched high above
Waiting to fall.
He is a thousand things,
For he is legion.

FEAR OF KNOWING

The plastic chair creaks
Under my weight,
Threatening to self-destruct
If I do not keep still.
The woman in front of me –
A scarecrow of skin and bones –
Blank look on her face,
Mouthing words I fail to hear.
The man beside her,
Slender arms mapped with
Rivers of bluish veins
Visible through pasty skin.
A fly lands on a festering ulcer.
Old man swipes a hand and
The buzzing intruder takes flight,
Only to land once more
On the same site.
What's the use?
All of us like suspects
In a police line, awaiting verdict.
My hand tightens around
Sealed, white envelope.

Too frightened to look,
Too terrified to know.
What's the use?
A door opens, and a young woman
Flaunting health
Calls my name.
The doctor will see you now.

MIDNIGHT SERENADE

Pitched tent
Under clear evening sky.
Dawn hours away,
Lake surface mirrors
Moon and starlight.
Crickets lend their
Collective voice –
A high-pitched, repetitive
Serenade
In the dim glow cast
By the dying embers
Of a campfire.
A crack of firewood.
A Coleman.
Beer can guzzles its
Foamy contents
Onto the ground.
The insects' performance ebbs
And grinds to an
Abrupt halt
With the blow of a hatchet.

IF YOU'RE COLD, THEY'RE COLD

Closed shutters
And latched windows.
Wooden chair braced
Against front door.
Glacial winds batter the landscape.
Boughs hang low,
Burdened by sleet,
Frozen into submission.
Crowd gathers 'round log cabin.
Blood stains winter wonderland.
Dead eyes peek
Through wooden slats;
Cold fists pound
In chaotic cadence.
Man crouches beside the
Fireplace, clutching axe.
He gazes at the door,
Eyes wild,
Realizing he shouldn't
Have gotten the locks
Made in China.

SOUP KITCHEN

The soup is thin and bland,
And no matter what's in it –
Carrots, cabbage,
Onions, or a little pork –
It always tastes like
Warm seawater.
That never stops them
From coming by the hordes;
Skin and bones
And hardly any more.
Supplies thin,
Close to spent.
Starving mouths;
Tongues licking spoons
And bowls clean.
Yet, no one speaks of
The occasional disappearances
And the rare instances
When the soup tastes
Absolutely divine.

A SPECIAL OCCASION

Laughter fills the brightly lit hall.
Glasses clink,
And men and women
Exchange handshakes
And pecks on the cheek,
Flashing smiles and
Rows of perfectly capped teeth.
Low-cut dresses
Hardly conceal breasts with
More lifts than the interstate.
Excited chatter about supper;
Ladies giggle in anticipation.
Dinner bell rings.
I try to scream,
But my lips are stitched shut,
And the guests are hungry.

WORKING MY WAY TO YOU

I walk into my apartment,
Reaching for the light switch.
Hum of electricity.
Your gazes fall upon me
From the walls of every room,
Watching my every move
The way I want you to as I
Work my way to you.
I set my bag on the bed,
Under your constant scrutiny.
I sit.
Rumpled sheets.
My hand draws the string
And reach in the bag,
Past bowie knife and Beretta
And pulls out leather notebook.
I take a pen from the nightstand.
Red ink, like a slice
Across an exposed neck,
Crosses out another name,
Drawing me closer to you.

S.O.B.

Like vermin on rafts,
They arrive by the boatload –
Russians, Asians, Europeans,
Americans, Latinos.
The first day is like show and tell,
Like listening to brats
Bragging on and on about
Some award they won in school,
As if that entitles them to something.
Gangsters, swindlers, hustlers,
Murderers, blasphemers,
Smugglers, defilers, killers,
And politicians.
They act all badass,
And that is all right;
Pride is one of the reasons
They're in my neighbourhood,
My neck of the woods.
By the end of the week,
Most of them are broken
In mind and spirit.
They claw at each other

And at themselves,
Tearing flesh and gouging eyes,
Peeling the skin off their faces.
That's always the entertaining part.
Occasionally, there is one guy
Who thinks he can run
The show better.
Pride, you see.
He comes to me,
Greed in his eyes, and points
At my throne and my crown.
I am all too happy to oblige.
Examples have to be made.
A badass he may be,
But I am the meanest motherfucker
To set foot in this pit.
My Father once said so himself.

ROASTING MARSHMALLOWS

Evening sky.
A streak across the heavens.
A falling star.
Quick! Make a wish.
Some ask for love,
Others, for fortune.
Many pray for a promotion,
A new iPhone,
Or a slim figure.
All fine and good,
Yet I am left to wonder
As a giant rock
Hurled from space
Plummets through the atmosphere,
How many people wish
It doesn't smash into
The planet's surface,
And cause global extinction.

CTRL, ALT, DELETE

We plugged them into our walls,
In our offices and our homes,
Like unborn infants
Drawing life through
Umbilical cords of insulated wiring.
We trusted them with our
Money, our safety,
Our communications,
And our darkest secrets.
Eventually, we relied
More on them
Than they did on us.
We were the ones
Who were obsolete –
The beepers, Betamaxes,
Cassette tapes of society.
It was only a matter of time
Before an update was necessary.

CATCH

Miles away from shore,
Two men who have fallen
Overboard
Bob like apples in a barrel.
Salty waters surround them –
A rolling topaz carpet
Stretching as far as
The eye can see.
On the deck, urgent cries;
Crew scrambles to
Throw distressed men a line.
Hunting grounds.
Both men paddle for the boat,
Fighting the ocean current
Eager to draw them
Farther away.
Fingernails claw the side
Of the fishing vessel
But acquire no purchase.
As the relentless waves
Slap the duo like vengeful
Wives exacting punishment

Onto lying spouses,
The men onboard finally manage
To lower a line.
Nearest man clutches lifeline;
And he would later tell
His companions
Not even the devil himself
Could pry it loose.
As they raise him and
Haul him on the deck,
The captain yells and points
To the icy waters.
A giant splash and a
Glimmer of scales.
The wretched scream that
Would haunt him to his grave.

FLUTTER

Alone on a park bench,
Cup of coffee by my side.
A flutter of wings
Behind me –
Hushed,
Barely noticeable.
It's time to go home.
I can't help but grin.
They are bound by rules
Whereas I am not.
Not yet, I say. I like it here.
I have things to do.
You've done enough.
Is that what He says?
Haven't you heard?
I'm in the details.
Another beating of wings.
This is not a request.
I will leave when I'm
Good and ready.
More wings.
They've surrounded me now.

I stare at my cooling
Drink and sigh.
Fine. But you asshats
Owe me a cup of coffee.

RICHTER (1257 A.K.)

Vehicles clog the streets
Like hair on a shower drain.
Motorists take
To the streets.
The chatter of gunfire
And grenades shake the city.
Screams drown
Wail of sirens;
Smouldering buildings
Billow black smoke
That choke the skies.
Emergency services
Scramble to aid
The fallen and wounded.
Citizens march like
Wildebeests to the bridge
Attempting to escape the city.
Mothers hug their infants;
Teachers herd their flock;
Men tell their sons to be brave.
Military trucks roll past
Blockades.

Soldiers disembark,
Faces ashen,
Fear written all over.
Lock and load,
For country and for
The human race.
Kaiju season has begun.

LOSING IT

He's been to three doctors,
And they all say the same thing:
All you need is rest;
It's just stress.
Bunch of hacks
With their college degrees!
They put their diplomas
With their fancy frames
Up on their clinic walls
And pretend to know everything.
How the hell do they expect
Him to rest when he
Cannot sleep?
The pills don't work;
He's even tried doubling the dose
On the sly.
Nada, kaput.
And alcohol only makes him sick.
Half the time, he doesn't
Know what day it is.
His clothes barely fit;
He's lost his appetite

And so much weight.
A knock on the apartment door.
It's Terry again,
Checking up on him.
At least he's got a friend.
Whatever he's got,
It'd be horrible to bear
His condition alone.
Terry cheers him up.
Christ, man, you look like shit.
Honesty is a good quality
For a friendship.
As they sit on the dusty couch,
Watching the ballgame,
He turns to Terry and asks
A question that's been
Bugging him the past couple
Of days.
Hey, didn't you die
In a car accident in high school?
Terry smiles and winks.
What are you talking about?
Game's about to start.
You're crazy, bro.

IN SICKNESS AND IN HEALTH,

'TIL DEATH

He browses
The large glass counter
As the female attendant waits,
Smiling dutifully.
So many to choose from;
All so expensive.
Not that he couldn't
Afford one;
Sure, some were well-above
His price range, and
Others were too flashy,
But before he'd walked in,
He told himself he wouldn't
Leave without one
For his wife –
One absolutely perfect.
He sighed, tired.
This was harder than
When he bought

Her engagement ring years ago.
The attendant coughs
As if to say,
"Come on! Pick!
I haven't got all day."
Guns.
Who knew purchasing
A murder weapon
Would be so difficult?

BETTER LATE THAN NEVER

Driving for hours;
Spring in the seat jabs his back,
Like being held at knifepoint
By a kidnapper.
Damn upholstery.
Been meaning to look into that;
Just like he'd have to
Look into his blood sugar
And blood pressure.
He shook his head in shame.
Procrastination would be
The death of him.

The truck wobbles on the dirt road.
He checks his watch
And curses.
His armpits are damp with sweat,
And the air-conditioning
Isn't helping one bit.
He looks out the windshield,

Trying to find a landmark,
Something to reassure him
He's on the right path.
What if he missed a turn?
Should he head back?
He adjusts the settings
On the dashboard
And thinks the AC is broken.

He eyes the rear view mirror
And eases off the gas,
Careful his cargo doesn't
Fall out the back.
He finally spots a man
Walking his dog up ahead –
A strange sight in
The middle of nowhere.
Cute dog though.
A terrier of some sort –
A hairy throw pillow.
He taps the brakes,
Eases to the right, and
Stops beside master and pet.

Dog owner shakes his head
And points back the way
He came.
He missed that turn after all;
Missed it by a long shot.
The driver groans.

Client's not going to be happy,
And in this business,
A satisfied customer
Is a regular customer.
"What are you delivering anyway?"
And before he knows
What's happening,
The busybody lifts the tarpaulin
Off his cargo.

Setting sun, elongating shadows.
He checks the time and knows
His delivery is overdue.
Tardiness is always
Bad for business.
Beside him, the little dog yips
And lolls its pink tongue.
Cute fella.
Definitely a terrier.
Back of the truck,
Cargo sealed once more.
His client might throw a fit,
But he hopes the extra body
Will more than make up
For lost time.

FLAT

No other vehicle in sight.
Dusk approaching;
Don't want to get stuck
Out here alone
When night comes.
He pops open the trunk
And retrieves the jack.
Takes a while to find
The tire iron and flashlight.
He rolls up his sleeves
And gets to work.
A sound in the distance.
Glances over his shoulder,
But nothing's there.
Jack in position;
Thirty seconds to lift the car.
Glad he's in shape.
Another sound.
Closer.
Like the snapping of a twig.
He grabs the flashlight
And pans the beam left and right.

Just trees and darkness.
Heart quickens,
Goosebumps on his arm.
Feeling of being watched.
He sets the torch on the ground
And loosens the first nut.
The wheel turns.
Something jutting out from
Between the treads
Catches his attention.
He grasps the object
Between his thumb and forefinger,
Holds it in front of his face.
Odd.
Some sort of sharpened fragment
Made of bone.
Shadow falls over him,
Followed by another sound
Directly from behind.

THICKER THAN WATER

Dawn
A few minutes away.
In the middle of the clearing,
Bound against
Large, wooden pillar,
Face against the timber,
So close, I can detect
The sweetish-sour scent
Of resin from the proud tree
From which this pillar
Was fashioned.
Hands outstretched,
Tied in front of me
In a manner that binds
While inflicting the most pain
And misery.
I have plenty of both,
But my captors seem
To think otherwise.
I suffer the burning lash
Of the whip on my back.
I feel my flesh tear and can only

Imaging the crisscross pattern
These artists of agony
Have created.
Tell us where your brothers are,
They demand
And promise no more harm
Will befall me once I give them
The information.
I smell deceit on them,
Wafting from their pores
And keep my mouth shut,
For I am neither a traitor nor
A simpleton.
A deafening shriek from
The tree line.
A dozen more answer.
My brothers have arrived.
The startled men grip their rifles,
Form a protective circle
Around the dwindling campfire.
The sunlight kills us,
And dawn is just minutes away.
But it is more than enough time,
As my captors
Are about to find out.

SECOND GENESIS

A thousand
Iron-clad angels
Rain down like tears
From the heavens.
History has a way
Of repeating itself,
And maybe we were living
Off borrowed time.
Inevitability.
It took forty days of rain
To wash away
The sins of our ancestors,
A flood which only served
To wipe the slate
For newer atrocities.

FRONTLINE

On the battlefield,
You wield your sword
Not for country;
Not for any flag,
Religion, or ideology.
You fight for the brother
Beside you;
You fight so you may return
To your wife and daughter,
So you may look into
The proud eyes of your son
Without flinching
And hope the war is over
Before his services
Are required.
Night is upon you,
And the air is cold.
The ground is slick
With the blood of
Comrade and foe.
Your breath plumes
And vanishes,

Fleeting, like your
Very existence in this world.
The enemy's forces crest
The hilltop,
Eyes glowing like windows
Looking into Hades.
Steady your blade;
Bring to mind why you fight,
And remember
The adversary's weakness
Is its head and throat.

WET MARKET

The air has a peculiar
Dampness to it,
As if all the odours congealed
And decided to throw up
On each other.
Two women argue
Over the cost of a slab
Of rotting meat.
I carry my purchase
By my side,
Haste in my step.
My rattan basket
Weighs heavily on my left arm.
In the dirt,
A child –
Festering wound on its arm –
Plays with a pair of bones.
It looks up at me with
Milky eyes
And goes back to
Its imaginary game.
Looks like the vertebrum

Was winning.
I hurry along;
There are hungry mouths to feed.

ABOUT THE POET

Aurelio Rico Lopez III is a self-diagnosed horror fanatic and scribble junkie. He is the author of several books, novellas, and poetry collections, including *Old School* (Azoth Khem Publishing), *Raising Hell* (Stitched Smile Publications), *Valhalla Falling* (Great Old Ones Publishing), *Zombies Don't Knock* (Night Horse Publishing House), *No Grave Too Deep* (SST Publications), *Food for the Crows* (Crowded Quarantine Publications), and *The Odd Ones* (Azoth Khem Publishing), to name a few. He is also the author of the haiku collection *Abra Cadaver* (Alban Lake Publishing). Aurelio hails from Iloilo City, Philippines.

ABOUT THE ARTIST

The street artist who goes by the name **Chipe** hails from Iloilo City, Philippines. His work never fails to provoke thought, stir emotions, and inspire. A devout student of the arts, he hopes one day you'll come visit Ill City where street art is alive and well.

Other poetry titles from HellBound Books for your delectation…

DARK MUSINGS

Available at www.hellboundbookspublishing.com

Dark Musings by Xtina Marie

The perfect companion piece to Light Musings – The dark side of Xtina Marie's poetry delves into intense emotions: heartache, loss, hurt, pain, rage, and a dangerous consuming love which can drive one insane. Dark Musings is not a collection!

The author returned to the centuries old practice of Narrative Poetry—the telling of a story through poetry. If you believe you are brave enough to explore the savage emotions of the human heart; Dark Musings will test your mettle.

LIGHT MUSINGS

Available at www.hellboundbookspublishing.com

Light Musings by Xtina Marie

The perfect companion piece to Dark Musings – an intriguing mirror image of the darkness you have just read, but no less deep and soul stirring.

What a web she weaves. Light Musings is a poetic narrative—a story told through related poems. Xtina Marie is a master of this style. Known by her fans as the Dark Poet Princess, this term of endearment came about as a result of the horror genre embracing her first book: Dark Musings which continues to garner stellar reviews. Light Musings will not disappoint her loyal fans as darkness is present within these pages as well. However, this latest book will show a much larger audience that Xtina's poetry pulls out every feeling the reader has ever experienced—forcing them to feel with her protagonist. Light Musings shows us that love is made from darkness and light; something Xtina Marie explores like no one else.

**A HellBound Books LLC
Publication**

www.hellboundbookspublishing.com

Printed in the United States of America

EBONY'S PROTECTOR

J THOMPSON

USA TODAY BESTSELLING AUTHOR

Ebook publication update-2021

Editor: Stephanie Farrant

Cover Design Fantasia Frog Designs

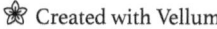 Created with Vellum

ABOUT THE BOOK

Ebony's Protector
(Previously released As Ebony)

Blurb
One sister born of pain.
One sister born of blood.
One sister born of death.

Three sisters bound,
Wiccan and vampire.
Three sisters found,
To join an empire.
A prophecy of three,
So let it be.

Ebony's life varied from minor inconvenience to total disaster. She could never catch a break. From a young age, she had been sent to live with many foster families, each one rejecting her after a short amount of time, none of them wanting to take on her unusual health issues.

She couldn't blame them; she didn't know what the hell was wrong with her, either. All she knew was that she'd been like this for as long as she could remember.

But is she ready to know the truth of her creating? Does she really need to answer all the unspoken questions in her mind?

With only her name and the leather tag around her wrist, Ebony fights her way to the answers of who - and what - she is. And whether she's ready for it or not, she's about to find the whole ugly truth of it.

PROLOGUE

THE MOONLIGHT'S silver rays beamed down on Angelica as another wave of pain crashed through her body. Her screams were muffled by the handle of an old hammer that had been placed in her mouth. Her long canines had pierced the wood hours ago. The change had torn through her body in reaction to the trauma she was going through—Angelica had no other word to describe what was happening right now.

She was giving birth.

And to no ordinary child. She was giving birth to a hybrid—a baby whose very existence was against the rules of all the immortal groups. Especially the secluded night-walkers. It was an unspoken understanding amongst all immortals that a mix of the races was just not done.

ngelica had fallen for a warlock. And not just any warlock, but the leader of his kind. Only, he hadn't fallen for her. He had merely used her

unique gifts **as a nightwalker queen,** used her **pure** blood, and her body.

Fortunately, Gregori had no idea that she had been pregnant when she had left his coven. She wouldn't have been able to leave so easily if he had.

Her own kind had ordered her to abort, but she couldn't bring herself to do it, no matter how scared and alone she felt. As the last member of the royal family, a lot rested on her shoulders, including the future of her line. But the child Angelica held inside her could be the key to stopping the immortal war. Could be the key to peace.

Another wave of pain punched through Angelica, forcing her body upright. She fought to keep from spitting out the wood and vomiting what little she had in her stomach.

"My lady,"

a gentle voice called from between her splayed legs. Rema, her lady-in-waiting and closest friend, looked up at her with worried eyes. Angelica was already aware that things were not going well, and a part of her had accepted that she may not survive the labour. But, for her, what mattered most was the life of her child.

"My lady, push. Please push,"

Rema urged. Angelica bent her head, focusing on what she needed to do, and gripped the sodden bed sheets until her knuckles turned white. Unlike the bed in her home, the one on which she now laid was nothing more than piles of old sheets— not made of silk or satin but ripped, dirty cotton—and polystyrene. The room was no more splendorous. In fact, it was hidden within the confines of an industrial building. It was dark and cold, the sunlight unable to penetrate the stone walls, but it kept her and her

unborn baby hidden from the from the prying eyes of the world.

Due to her kind being against the birth, she'd had no choice but to deliver her baby in hiding, with only two trusted people aware of where she was. She didn't doubt that once her child was born, her race would welcome it. They would do so unwillingly, but her child would be a royal, after all, and that was a title they could grudgingly respect. But she hadn't wanted to take the chance of them having access to her when she was at her weakest.

Gentle hands cupped her shoulders and urged her to lean back against a hard chest. Her bodyguard, Nathaniel, smiled at her, his own canines only just visible showing he, too, was a true nightwalker. He was a member of her elite guard and as close to her as a male could get to a royal. He was like a brother. His deep voice and kind eyes helped her.

"Come on, Angel," he urged. "You can do this."

Bowing her head once again, her teeth cutting through part of the wood, Angelica bared down, pushing with all her might to expel the life within her. She felt her body give way, freeing the small form of her child. Only its small choking cry gave her any hint of its health. Before she could ask to hold her baby, another wave of pain erupted through her.

This time, her scream filled the room as the wooden handle fell to the floor. The clattering of wood on concrete was drowned out by Angelica's panting.

"What's happening?" she asked, worry lacing her words.

Her body felt out of her control, as if something had given way. She had felt weak before, but now she had become lethargic. The urge to close her eyes was as intense as the pain that flowed through her. Only Rema's voice kept her conscious.

"My lady, keep pushing," her lady in waiting softly urged, but Angelica didn't miss the panic in her voice.

"What's wrong?" Nathaniel asked, and gave a comforting squeeze to Angelica's shoulders.

Rema looked up.

"Your daughter is fine, my lady, but she is not alone," her timid voice answered. "I see another head. Please, my lady, you have to keep pushing."

Her plea shocked Angelica, so much so that instead of replying, she simply nodded and pushed. Her head swam as a wave of dizziness hit her, but still she kept on pushing, until another wave of intense pain and then immediate relief and release rushed through her. The sound of something popping was ignored as another cry from an infant's mouth filled the empty room.

Angelica smiled, her head spinning and her words slurred as she called out,

"Rema." Angelica, exhausted, laid back against Nathaniel's chest.

"Another girl, my lady."

"Good," Angelica whispered, and started to close her eyes, her strength waning. She felt herself being lowered to the makeshift bed. Two babies were a blessing—twins were a rarity, and as such, would cement their safety with her race.

She felt so tired. Her body was sluggish in responding to her demands. Laying her head to the side, she watched as Nathaniel approached with two small bundles in his hands.

One head with golden locks could be seen, and another with red. Her daughters: the start of a new beginning for the immortals.

"Beautiful," she whispered.

She had done it—brought a new life into the world. Not one, but *two* females that would lead their race into a new era. Angelica wished with everything she had left that she would be able to watch them grow. Watch them blossom.

"They shall be named Scarlett and Ivory," she whispered.

Angelica closed her eyes. She had lost the feeling in her legs, and the numbness was slowly travelling up her body. Taking with it her life and essence.

Her time had come.

"Beautiful," she whispered again as she closed her eyes for the last time.

~

Rema, lady in waiting to the last royal of the nightwalkers—vampires, as the human race liked to call them—looked up into the sad gaze of Nathaniel, leader of the elite guard, and her brother. In his arms lay the future, ones they would both protect with their lives.

"My lady," she called out, touching the hand of the queen she had served for a century.

Only her skin had cooled, and she no longer felt a heartbeat.

"Angelica?"

Heart racing, Rema leant over her queen, her eyes searched her face. She looked for any sign that her assump-

tion was wrong. That her friend was not, in fact, passing over.

"No, no, no," she sobbed, and shook the queen.

"No, you cannot be dead, Angelica," she shouted, and shook her again.

"You are stronger than this, dammit." Rema choked back her sobs as she finally admitted that their queen was gone. The second birth, she could only conclude, had caused a significant amount of bleeding that they had no hope of stopping. The queen's healing abilities should have stopped it, but if it had, it had been too late.

"Nathan." She called her brother over, although there was no need. He hadn't missed her cries. He had just given her a moment to mourn.

"She's gone." Her voice cracked as emotion threatened to take over once again. She watched as he walked back over to the basket where the heirs to the nightwalker throne now lay, and tucked a blanket around them. They had been prepared for only one child, yet now they had two.

She watched as her brother knelt beside her. Taking her hand in his, he bowed his head. He whispered the vow every nightwalker guard swore when assigned to their charge, his voice hoarse with emotion as tears fell to the cold concrete.

"I vow by my blood to serve and protect. My life for yours. Always.

Rema fought back her tears. She had to keep busy. She couldn't stop and think. Not when two tiny lives now depended on her. Rema moved to start cleaning Angelica, wanting to give her as much dignity as possible, only to see a crown of dark hair part-breached from the queen.

"Nathan!" she cried out, her hands moving to touch the head. They had little time to lose. "Nathan, there's a third,"

she shouted again, and her own shocked expression met that of her brother's.

"We need to get it out." She looked at her queen, then back to her brother, knowing what was to come. "We need to get it out. Now."

"Please forgive us, Angelica," Rema whispered as Nathan pulled a dagger free. Regret flashed across his face before he nodded and bent to his task.

Yes, Angelica, Queen of the nightwalkers, was dead.

But...

Three lives had come at the cost of one.

The prophecy had been born.

1
_____

Twenty-two years later...

The loud drip of water hitting ceramic echoed throughout the small bathroom. The tiles were aged, the grout no longer a bright white but instead a sickly, dull grey. Most played host to a myriad of cracks, many of the corners completely broken away. The linoleum floor was also cracked, the edges raised, peeling from the concrete below.

Out of the six cubicles, only three had functioning doors, but the people that used these facilities took no notice—too drunk to care about strangers seeing them do their business. The bathroom had a constant smell of urine, which someone had attempted to mask with the sweet scent of potpourri. Ebony had grown accustomed to the odour. Although, at first, it had made her gag.

Splashing her face with the cold water, she looked at her reflection through the cracked and frosted mirror. She wasn't much to look at; sickly pale skin, black circles under her drab grey eyes, prominent cheek bones—all reflecting just how shitty she was feeling. She always felt shitty, had

for as long as she could remember. Her whole life had been plagued with illness after illness.

First, she had been told she had anaemia. She took the news well, knowing it could be dealt with easily by regularly taking iron tablets. She began to resent her illness, however, when her first foster family refused to pay for her medication, when they looked at her as though she was a burden. They soon sent her back to the foster home. Then she was diagnosed with photophobia, which gradually got worse as she got older. Another foster family hadn't wanted to deal with her health problems, so back to the home she went. Ebony suffered with other issues as well, but by the time she turned eighteen, she'd saved all the money she had earned from her part-time job waiting on tables at the local pub, packed her things and caught the first train out of the tiny town of Verwood. The town had done nothing but make her feel more and more like she didn't fit in. She had always been an outsider.

Pulling an old t-shirt from her rucksack, Ebony used it to dry her face. Then she changed from the vest top and jeans she'd been wearing to another identical set. They were the only clothes she owned, and all she could do was wash them in the same sink she had just washed herself.

She once again looked at herself in the mirror, whilst fingering the small leather tag she had around her wrist. No fine jewellery for her. This shabby, unadorned bracelet was all she had left of her family that had left her to die as a baby. Why she kept it, she didn't know, but every time she had thought about throwing it away, she hadn't been able to go through with it.

Life had decidedly been shite from the moment she had been found lying in a pile of ash and screaming like a banshee. So she'd been told. Not that she believed

anything anyone said to her anymore. She still didn't know whether she believed her father had been a smackhead who left her for dead, that he was the origin for all her health issues.

Being informed she was a screw-up at every turn had eventually convinced her of her own uselessness. So here she was, four years after escaping Verwood, finding herself trapped by her own pathetic life. No home, poor health, and a job that paid just enough to get her the iron tablets she needed. Food had become a luxury for her, something she needed and wanted but couldn't always obtain.

Ebony packed her rucksack and turned back to her reflection. She tied her long raven hair into a loose braid, ignoring the pang of pity that settled in her stomach. What did feeling sorry for yourself get you but another boot up the arse and ridicule.

"Come on, Ebs, another day survived."

She sighed, the sound of her own voice making her wince. Even noise had become an issue, her hearing far too sensitive for her own good. It was making her current job at the bar harder and harder to deal with.

Unfortunately, Ebony had no choice.

This job was all she had. This was where—much to the owner's ignorance—she slept as well. Not that she slept well.

Ebony had somehow managed to keep it quiet that she was sleeping on the old, worn couch in the staff room, and that she washed every day in the dingy customer toilets. But it was getting more and more difficult to pretend that everything was okay when it clearly wasn't. Ebony had no friends and no family.

She was alone.

"Ebony," a deep voice called. "You here?"

Slipping her jacket over her shoulders, she picked up her rucksack before replying as she exited the toilets.

"Yes, Barney, I'm here, just dumping my bag in the staff room." Her voice sounded weak, but she ignored it, instead walking out into the club to see the lights now on and the DJ starting his nightly routine of setting up.

"Evening, Ebony."

"Hey, Buster," she replied, and waved. The people she worked with were friendly, but still she didn't feel like she belonged. Dumping her bag in its usual place in the staff room, she walked back towards the bar. This was her life; working behind the bar, trying to sleep in the staff room, washing in a dirty bathroom, and repeat.

This was all she knew: serving drinks and dealing with obnoxious punters.

"No more breakages tonight, please, Ebony," Barney's voice sounded from his office behind the bar. He had been the owner and manager of *The Back Door* for as long as anyone could remember. Everyone she had asked had stated as much, but that had been all they had divulged—again, a sure sign that she didn't belong. She merely existed.

"Yes, Barney," she answered, and continued setting up the bar. Her actions became automatic; taking glasses from the washer and placing them back on the shelves; removing old optics and changing them for new ones; restocking the fridges.

The Back Door wasn't a classy place and, as such, didn't attract classy clientele. Ebony wasn't fussed—it wasn't as if she was anything special. The only booze available was either beer, vodka or whiskey. That was it. Not a lot to remember, or get wrong.

She just had to remember to not drop any more glasses.

．　．　．

Looking at the small black clock that was hidden under the top of the bar, Ebony sighed. Eight p.m.: time to open.

"I'm gonna open up, Barney, you know, for the masses." Buster smirked at her sarcasm from his place behind DJ booth, and started to play a deep bass that reverberated from the speakers and made Ebony feel like it was coming from her chest. The music choices were always dubious, and some pushed the boundaries to the point of making her ears bleed.

Unlocking all the bolts on the non-descript black door, she opened it briefly, looking outside into the dull evening. The sound of the normal Friday night London traffic could be heard, along with the laughter and footsteps of people milling around. She breathed in the night air, letting it fill her lungs. Eyes closed, she tilted her head to the sky.

"Fuck my life," she released on a sigh. "Fuck it to hell." Desperation laced her words. She clenched her fist at her side and scraped the nails of her other hand against the wood of the door as she held it open. Her head still raised to the sky, she looked up at the stars, the night cool and clear. "My life sucks."

Ebony turned back into the bar that had become her temporary home and wondered if life could possibly get any worse.

Surely, she had already hit rock bottom.

2
_____

Nathaniel, Captain of the Nightwalker Guard, was bone-tired. His muscles ached, his eyes were sore, and his head throbbed with every beat of his heart. He wished he could blame it on the rigorous training with his guardsmen, or fighting rogues, or even warlocks.

Nope.

He was fed up with not only dealing with the politics of his race, but also babysitting the two beings that required his and the guards' constant protection, though regularly threw it back in their faces. His two charges had been as such since the day they were born Princesses of the night-walker race. They were royalty. Revered and protected. They were also spoiled brats that needed more than watching over.

Hell, if he had his way, he would have them both chained in their rooms and the doors locked. Ever since they had reached what humans would call maturity, they had been nothing but trouble. Constantly escaping their royal quarters to visit the human clubs and 'party' with no thought as to what their actions would do or how it would

look to the race. That and they were not as safe as they thought out there in the big, wide world. Little did they know that not all races revered the nightwalker royal family.

Nathan scrubbed a hand down his face before he once again looked at the summons from the council. Every immortal race had a council, a chosen few who represented their race and also dealt with any justice and punishment that the guard were unable to deal with. Nathan read the words once again, and winced. They had called for the princess's to be present at the next meeting. A meeting that would decide their fates as royals.

Or more bluntly put, their marriages. The council were fully aware that the girls were not full-blooded nightwalkers, but they were royal, which meant, unfortunately, their lives were not their own. What the council was not aware of was there should have been a third.

The memory of having to leave both his queen and her third stillborn child had eaten at him for years. Perhaps if they had been quicker, they may have saved her. His queen, in her final moments, had given life to three beautiful girls, fulfilling an ancient prophecy that was quickly ended when Rema, his sister, had realised there was no life in the third child. One born with hair the colour of night. A true contrast to her sisters—one blonde and one red.

"May the goddess forgive me," Nathan whispered, as he always did when he thought of that sad day. He again looked at the summons, his thoughts going to the possible reaction of the girls. Those two had mouths on them, and they wouldn't be afraid to voice their opinions.

"Well *that's* going to go down like a lead fucking balloon," he ground out, and looked up at the security monitors that covered the wall in front of his desk. The glare from the screens didn't help his growing headache.

All aspects of the property were covered, from the driveway that led to the front door all the way around to the small garden at the rear. Being in the capitol meant there wasn't much space outside, but they had made do with what they had. Refurbished to the highest standard, Nathan took his job, and the protection of his charges, seriously. A movement on his monitor warned him of a new visitor moments before a loud knock sounded on the door.

"Come," was all he said, tidying the papers in front of him. Nathan leaned back to regard the nightwalker that entered. Bishop had served their race almost as long as he had. He was one of the largest males of their kind. Most of the other guards joked he had been born with berserker blood, although that was an impossibility for his kind. No matter the race of the mother, the child took after the sire, especially if he was a nightwalker. Still, Nathan had his suspicions. Despite those suspicions, Bishop was also Nathan's friend and second in command.

He watched as Bishop folded his huge arms across his chest and huffed out a breath.

"Bishop," Nathan acknowledged.

"What's happened now?" he asked, already knowing the answer. Bishop only got agitated about one thing, and it happened to be female, blonde, and a princess.

"The usual," was all the answer Bishop gave. The proud warrior dipped his chin to his chest and let another sigh leave him. "I swear she's going to be the fucking death of me."

"Both of them managed to get out again?"

The warrior nodded, letting his hands fall to his sides, his fists clenched, before Bishop's bright blue eyes met his own, the luminescent colour showing how on the edge his

second in command was. That concerned Nathan, but he would have to worry about that at another time.

Holding his hand up, he stopped Bishop from leaving. "I will go this time, my friend," he stated simply, and picked up his leather jacket from the back of his chair. "I need the air, and you need the break from their attitudes."

"I swear, if I catch her, I won't be responsible for my actions, Nathan. She's pushed me too far this time."

Nathan slipped his arms into his jacket and looked— really looked—at his friend. The lines of strain were evident. He didn't ask what she had done this time. He only knew that Ivory made it her personal mission to wind Bishop up.

"You would harm a royal?" Nathan asked, knowing the warrior wouldn't, but still wanting confirmation.

"Hurt her?" he repeated as he opened the door. He walked through, before he stopped and turned his head. "I would never hurt her, Nathan. I couldn't. But that doesn't stop me from wanting to put her over my knee and spanking that royal arse of hers."

Nathan's eyebrows shot up as his friend left the office, leaving him with a mental image he most certainly didn't want. Slipping his daggers into their sheaths under his arms, Nathan headed out into the night to start his search for not one, but two of most annoying and beautiful women he had ever known.

～

Retrieving two beautiful women on a Friday night in London would have been, to most, a daunting task—possibly an enjoyable one if they were not heirs to the throne of their race—but Nathan was not your

average male, and as Captain of their elite guard, he was always willing and ready for a challenge. He had learned a long time ago to take many precautions with the princesses safety, and that meant, for starters, putting a tracker on their phones.

The girls had assumed the guard were still in the dark ages and would struggle to find them, which just showed their naivety, and gave Nathan an advantage. Placing trackers on their phones had been a no-brainer. Simple really.

Once they were back in the safety of the mansion, he would have to finally sit and talk to them. Too much relied on them, and he didn't need his entire guard putting in their notices because two royal brats were pissing them off.

Looking down at his own phone, he meandered in and out of the foot traffic, weaving around humans who didn't even look up to see where they were going. Their lives short and pathetic, they had no idea what creatures hunted the night. What they imagined—what they thought... it was nothing like their movies.

Seeing the final location beep on the map, he put his phone back into his pocket and turned down a side street. His eyes easily cut through the dimness of the night—only rodents and homeless dared venture down this route. His bright orbs were the only tell-tale sign of what he truly was: a hunter, a warrior, a nightwalker.

Nathan approached the non-descript black door that signalled the entrance to one of the few hangouts for immortals and demons. The strewed rubbish and strong smell of urine by back door confirmed this place was a hovel and definitely not somewhere Ivory or Scarlett should be visiting. They had more to worry about than simply clueless humans who didn't know who and what they were.

Checking his sheaths once again, Nathan pulled the door open easily, letting the hard bass of the music escape into the night before he slipped in quietly, letting the door close on its own. As soon as his eyes had adjusted to the dimness, he let his gaze sweep the room.

Easy as catching a mouse with cheese, he thought when he saw them. He had expected more of a fight.

"Easy-peasy."

3

THE NIGHT, unbelievably, had turned out to be not that bad, although Ebony had only been at the bar a few months. In that time, she had gotten to know the regulars, and she liked them. Even if they were strange as hell. It was also the first time in a while that she felt relatively normal. Not that she expected that to stay as it was. But she would gladly take even a few hours reprieve from feeling shitty.

"Another whiskey, Harry," she called out, already measuring out a double to serve the little, old man that propped up the bar. His warm smile forced one from her own lips as she slid the glass in front of him and took away his empty. The bar wasn't overly crowded—most of the customers had decided to sit in the booths at the back, nursing their drinks.

A few of the customers made the hairs on the back of her neck stand on end, as if in warning, but Ebony put that down to the location. It was something she would have to get used to. Shaking her head free of strange thoughts, Ebony busied herself cleaning the bar and collecting

glasses, until the door opened and in walked something new.

Two women. Two stunningly beautiful women. One a redhead, and the other a blonde, both dressed in long, fur-lined coats. Their heels clicked on the threadbare carpet that patchily covered the cement beneath. Their faces mostly covered by designer sunglasses, Ebony could almost taste the wealth.

Most of the customers also noticed and, strangely, sank back into their seats in an obvious effort to be ignored.

And ignored they were as the women made a beeline for the bar. Ebony forced a smile on her face as they perched on the rickety stools.

"Good evening." She smiled and tilted her head, a strange sense of familiarity hitting her.

"What can I get you?" Ebony asked, and waited for the women to acknowledge her presence. The silence they gave her made Ebony uncomfortable. As they lowered their sunglasses, she was shocked to see bright blue orbs shining back at her—assessing her.

"Wow—" Ebony started to say before her arm was grabbed and she was pulled to the side by Barney.

"What the fuck are you doing? Don't stare." His growl had Ebony frowning and looking up into the dark brown eyes of her boss. His large body was standing in front of her own, blocking the view of the women.

"Go to the cellar and get some fucking champagne," he ground out, his grip on her arm tightening, then turned his head and smiled sweetly at the two women who now had removed their coats and were making themselves comfy at the bar.

"We have champagne?" Ebony asked, a little stunned that a place that looked like it spawned the fleas on rats

could possibly be able to afford a luxury item like champagne. She watched, eyes wide in shock, as he lifted a chubby hand as if to slap her. Only the curt voice of one of the women stopped him.

"We are waiting," she snapped, and clicked her fingers.

He released her arm and pushed her towards the stairs that lead to the cellar. Ebony hated it down there. She always felt like she was being watched, and usually couldn't wait to leave as soon as possible. But this time, she didn't notice—too lost in her thoughts. No one, in her entire life, had gone to lift a hand to her. Even in the roughest foster homes, they had never dared—not with her health issues. But now, a man she thought better of, had proved her wrong. Finding a wooden crate at the back of the dingy cellar, Ebony wanted to hold her breath to prevent her from breathing in the putrid air of mould, damp, and what Ebony would describe as death.

The crate was nailed shut and showed that, yes, Barney had champagne, but he had never bloody opened the crate.

"Tight-arsed git," she mumbled as she found a crow bar and wedged it under the lid. A small shot of adrenaline helped her pry the lid open enough to pull a bottle through.

"I hope the cork hits him in the face," she grumbled again, and moved to go back up the stairs. As she cleared the top step, she nearly bumped into one of the customers leaving the men's bathroom.

"Oh, shit. Sorry." She smiled as she released her grip on his arm—where she had grabbed him in her fear of falling back down the stairs.

His grunt was her only answer, before he shucked her arm and stormed back off towards the bar.

"Oohkay. What the hell is up with everyone?" she whispered under her breath. She plastered a smile on her face as

she walked back behind the bar. Barney was right where she had left him, practically bowing to the women.

"Ah, Ebony, please hand me the bottle." Ebony did as asked, and then stepped back and out of the way, deciding that the bar needed a clean down. Preferably at the opposite end to her boss. His new suck-up attitude was out of place for a guy who never even served. In the months she had been at *The Back Door*, he had not once lifted a finger to help her, even when it had been busy.

Watching his actions made Ebony question the two new visitors. It seemed he was scared to displease them—even a little. Although, from the looks of them, they wanted for nothing. Both were dressed in dresses that would cost Ebony more than a year's wages, if not more. Hell, even their handbags were probably worth more than what Barney made in a year.

A hint of jealousy hit Ebony as she watched the women, wondering what it would be like to not have to worry about needing a place to stay, or where her next meal would come from. Even not having to worry about being able to afford her iron tablets would be a relief. Unfortunately, that's not something she would have the pleasure of feeling any time soon.

Without realising it, Ebony had been staring at the women and now had the returned gaze of the redhead. Her own bright blue eyes bored into Ebony, making her feel as if she was marked. That now she had unwittingly gained their attention, she wouldn't be able to get rid of it. Bowing her head, Ebony turned and focused on doing her job. The last thing she needed right now was to piss off a customer and, in turn, piss off Barney—who would have no issues with seeing her sacked.

She had the distinct feeling that he didn't really like her

but had employed her because no one else had applied for the job. Ebony wasn't a bad worker—hell, she worked damn hard and was always the first to arrive and last to leave. Even though the leaving part was up for interpretation.

"Ebony!" a sharp shout came, making her wince, and she lifted her head to look at Barney. He looked irritated, like someone had taken away his favourite toy. Placing the glass back on the counter, along with the cloth she and been using to wipe it, she walked over. Ebony managed a small smile as she approached.

"Yes, Barney, do you need anything?"

"Serve," he all but growled as he thrusted the now open bottle of champagne into her hands. Ebony fumbled for a moment, almost dropping the expensive bubbly, before she managed to get a grip and place it on the bar. Steeling herself, Ebony looked up and forced a smile.

"Hi," she blurted out, and was rewarded with a simple lift of the right eyebrow from the blonde. Ebony looked over the bar and saw that Barney had left nothing with which to drink the champagne from.

"I'm sorry, let me get some glasses," she rushed out, pushing the hair that had escaped from her braid behind her right ear, and his time, she got an answer.

"It's alright, honeybunch, take your time." Ebony lifted her head just over the edge of the bar from where she had knelt to look for any glass that would be suitable for the bubbly. The blonde had spoken, and now gave her a close-lipped smile. The redhead had her back to the bar and was watching the other customers.

"Nice bracelet," the blonde purred, and smiled again.

"Thank you," Ebony mumbled, and continued her search. Why Barney thought to buy champagne but not provide any bloody glasses for it, she didn't know. Instead,

she pulled out two half-pint glasses, smiling apologetically as she placed them on top of the bar and stood.

"Will these be ok?" she asked, then waited.

"Sure, they will do. Hey, Scar, you happy with a half-pint of champers?"

"Fuck yeah," was the only response

"Fill 'em up, honey."

Ebony nodded and proceeded to do as asked, gently pouring the bubbly liquid into the glasses before she slid them over the polished wood.

"Can I get you anything else?" she asked, unsure of what else two wealthy women could possibly want in a dive like *The Back Door*.

"Well," the blonde started, "let's start with your name."

"Ivory," the redhead called out, her tone full of warning

"Oh, shush, Scarlett." Ebony watched as something passed between them, their gazes locking for a few seconds before Ivory turned her eyes back to Ebony.

"It's Ebony," she replied. "Anything else?" she asked, not sure whether she liked their new-found interest in her. She had always been the one that blended into the background, not wanting to be noticed.

She liked it that way.

"Isn't that a pretty name," Ivory answered. "Well, I'm Ivory, and this is my sister, Scarlett."

Ebony nodded and picked up a cloth, needing to do something with her hands—anything to use as an excuse to get away from Ivory's piercing stare.

"Nice to meet you."

"Aww, ain't you sweet. So... what's that behind your ear? Is it a tattoo?" Ivory asked, then sipped her drink. Her eyes sparkled, reminding Ebony of the sea when the sun hits the surface.

Ebony unconsciously moved her hand up to her right ear, instead of pushing her head behind it she moved the strands forward before she shook her head.

"No, it's not a tattoo," she answered, then bent her head and moved to the other side of the bar, thankful another customer wanted a refill. The mark Ivory had seen was a birthmark behind her right ear. It was a dark brown and stood out on her pale skin. Most would ignore it if it was a normal birthmark, but it was in the shape of a perfect crescent moon, with the crescent facing the left.

Continuing to avoid the women. Ebony served her drinks, doing her best to stay off Barney's shit list for the evening. She didn't need anything bad happening, but her gut was saying her night would not end well.

The entrance door swung open again, gaining everyone's attention as a tall man walked in. Ebony's breath caught. He was gorgeous at well over six feet, with short brown hair, long enough to brush the nape of his neck. His nose fitted his profile to perfection, and his lips... although stretched into a harsh line, she guessed were soft and sin worthy.

His eyes, unusually, were the same shade of blue as Ivory and Scarlett, although he didn't look anything like them. She watched as he looked around the room, eyes taking in everything, until they fell, unsurprisingly, on the two women. The one named Ivory grinned when he started to walk over and nudged her sister.

Finally, they would hopefully leave, and Ebony could go back to hiding in the shadows.

4

NATHAN'S NOSE felt violated from the stench that erupted from the bar as he had opened the door. He couldn't pinpoint the exact smell that set his stomach on edge, but the overall effect made him wonder what, exactly, the girls thought about being in such a shithole.

He felt the stares of the other customers—hell, he even sensed it when they realised who and what he was. Some slid back further in to their seats, others blatantly got up and headed to the back, obviously in search of the rear exit.

His reputation always seemed to gain that reaction. He had been the leader of the Elite Guard for over two hundred years, a post he gained through his own blood and the blood of many foes. His queen had trusted him above everyone else to guard her, and then to guard her daughters. Although that task had turned out to be a damn sight harder than it had been guarding the queen.

He had spotted the two princesses as they perched against the bar with a bottle of champagne. That surprised him—champagne was the last drink he expected to see served in a place like *The Back Door*.

His nose twitched as a hooded figure slipped past the bar. *Werewolf.* They had a distinct smell and made him want to sneeze. After the figure had vanished from view, Nathan walked over to the bar. Both his charges looked out of place, their expensive clothing standing out in a room where even the carpet had given up to the wear and tear of decades of shoes shuffling across it.

His eyes met those of Scarlett, who's only response to his presence was a raise of an eyebrow. She had always been the most serious out of the two sisters. The one who thought first and acted later. Whereas Ivory, who still had her back to him, chatting to the bartender, was a lot more flighty and said whatever entered her head. She also had been the only one to ever wrap an elite guard around her finger, like she had Bishop.

"Scarlett," he said simply. Again, his answer was an action—a simple lift of the shoulders as she nodded her head to Ivory. A simple gesture that meant, *don't ask me, this was her idea.*

"Ivory, time to go," he said, and watched once again as Scarlett's eyes flickered, but this time they went to the girl behind the bar, the one who held Ivory's attention.

Flicking his gaze to her, he watched as she scuttled away, eager to be away from the sisters. Not that he could blame her. She was the same height as the girls, only she had deep, dark raven hair. Her eyes were a pale grey, and her skin tone was of a similar colour. This mortal was not well. She was beautiful, though.

But what did he care? He didn't. He needed to get the princesses out of the bar and back to the mansion, preferably without any of the other immortal races getting in the way.

He was already convinced he was too late to prevent that, but that didn't stop him from needing to get them away before others decided the girls were great targets for kidnap, extortion, and blackmail.

"Ladies, let's go," he growled out, and watched Ivory stand before she turned and poked him in the chest.

"You are an arse," she spat out. "Always ruining our fun."

"Fun... Really? In here?" he shot back.

"We were making friends," she answered, and fumbled in her purse for her phone.

"With the mortal? Great plan, Ivory." She growled again and looked to Scarlett, but Nathan continued before they could form an argument, "Come on, now. Besides, you have an apology to make."

"Oh, sod off. Bishop was being an arse, too." Ivory pouted. "He deserved it." She grinned, and Nathan felt for his friend.

"Enough," he snapped. "Let's go."

Turning, Nathan made to move. He wanted out of the bar and back to the mansion. He hadn't fed in a while and he felt on edge.

"Nathan." The deeper, husky sound of Scarlett had him turning.

"Not now," he threw across his shoulder. "Let's move. I'm fed up of your stunts. This time I'm telling the council. *They* can deal with you both."

He could tell by the sound of heels on cement that they were now following his lead. He could even hear the words falling from their lips as they called him all the names under the sun.

"Why you two seem to think it's ok and safe just to piss off and do your own thing is beyond me." Nathan turned on

them both. "Do either of you know how much danger you could be in?"

He waited, and they said nothing

"Seriously," he shouted, exasperated, and turned again. He headed towards the end of the alley and to the now waiting limo that had been sent as soon as he had located the girls.

"You are the last Royals. Without you, believe it or not, our race may resort to war to see a new ruling house reign."

Nathan gripped the door handle of the limo and wrenched the door open, holding it as he waited for them to enter.

"Is that what you want to see?" he asked and looked at them as they sat back in their seats. Only, he didn't see remorse for their actions; he saw anger that matched his own, and determination.

"What the fuck did you have to gain from coming here besides pissing off the guard?"

Nathan looked from one sister to the other and waited. It was Scarlett's deep voice that answered.

"We came here for our race, Nathaniel. We came here for our sister."

Nathan didn't have chance to close the door. Instead, it was pulled from his grasp by Scarlett, who slammed it with enough force it shook the limo.

Their words were slow to enter his brain.

How did they know? How had they found out? She was dead—had been for twenty-four years.

Nathan knew the limo had pulled away but made no move to follow. Instead, he looked back down the alley that lead to *The Back Door*. What had he missed?

A scream—one that was filled with fear—ripped

through the dark, and before Nathan knew what was happening, he was already racing towards the source.

"**S**carlett, why did you tell him? He's going to think *he* found her, not us," Ivory moaned. They had travelled to *The Back Door* on a tip-off from a shady imp that there was a mortal working there that smelled strange. She wasn't fully mortal—that was obvious. They didn't know what she was. Ivory and her sister had been following any lead they could since they had been told—by mistake—that there was, in fact, a third sister. They hadn't believed for one second that she was dead.

Since they had been old enough to communicate, they had known there was a bond. A bond that tied them. It was like a warm feeling in their chests, and there was no way it could be as strong as it was if all three of them weren't alive.

Rema, the woman they had always looked up to since they were young, had finally admitted that when they had been born, a third child had followed. But she had been stillborn, and due to the dawn breaking, they had made the choice to leave her with her mother, so they could face the sun together. Rema had described every detail of the child, even down to the small leather bracelet she had tied around her wrist. A gift for the dead.

"I told him because he needs to be the one to fetch her. You saw how skittish she was with us," Scarlett answered. "She doesn't know what we are, or even what she is. Dammit, Ivory, she's barely surviving."

Ivory nodded. When they had entered the bar, they had known from the first glimpse that she was their missing sister. Their features were the same, only their hair colour

was different, along with the birthmark. Each had a different phase of the moon—Scarlett had the opposite crescent moon to Ebony's, and Ivory had the full moon. This alone identified her as their sister, along with the feeling they had both got deep in their soul: that they had finally found her.

As a nightwalker, they could do things other races couldn't, but as a nightwalker hybrid—hybrid meaning Wiccan—you could say their skills were a little more advanced than even their guard, Nathan, was aware of. Foresight was Scarlet's gift, one she rarely tapped into out of fear of seeing a loved one harmed. But for this search, she had used it. Ivory's was slightly different, it combined with her nightwalker powers and made her exceptionally good at manipulation. Bishop, unfortunately, always seemed to be at the brunt of her experiments, but it meant they had been able to search and find the missing third of their family.

Both girls knew more than Nathan believed. They were aware of the council's need to control their actions, to control the race. They knew the council wanted to pair them off with their chosen males, who would then rule. They had both decided that would never happen. That once their sister was found, the race would be ruled by the royal princesses, whether the council liked it or not.

"But why Nathan? He's a brute and a pain in the arse. He's more likely to scare her off," Ivory whined.

"No, he won't." Scarlett grinned for the first time in a while. "Nathan is about to meet his match."

"Noooo." Ivory squealed and clapped, sounding more and more like a school girl gaining gossip than one who's race depended on her.

"Nathan will bring our sister home," she stated, and sat back in the plush leather seats. Ivory, who had the inability to sit still, looked at her phone once again, her fingers flying over the screen as she prepared for the long-awaited arrival of their sister. Clothing and other items ordered, she grinned and squealed once again.

"We found you, Ebony."

5

Ebony had watched the male as he approached the two women from the corner of her eye. She couldn't hear what was being said, but she could tell the girls weren't happy, and neither was he from the scowl that crossed his face.

Ignoring the obvious argument between the two, Ebony attempted to focus on her job and ignore the wooziness that was making an unexpected come back. This was why she needed her iron tablets. They seemed to be the only thing that stopped her from keeling over and passing out.

"Barney," she called out as she served another glass of whiskey to Harry in the corner. When he grunted in thanks, she smiled. Ebony moved over to the door of Barney's office and found him hiding in the corner, out of sight.

"Barney, you ok?" she asked.

"I'm fine," he snapped. "What do you want?" He sneered, but Ebony could see the sweat as it poured from his forehead.

"I'm just popping to the staff room to get something from my bag," she answered. "I'll only be two minutes."

"Fine, just hurry up. We don't have time for you to be slacking."

Ebony wanted to snap back that she never slacked. She was always the one that did the work whilst Barney sat on his lard arse doing nothing and shouting orders. His holier than thou attitude grated on every nerve Ebony had, and she itched to tell him to sod off, but she needed the job more than anything, so instead of snapping, Ebony smiled and nodded before she slid away from the bar and headed towards the staff room. The two women and the angry man were still there, but she ignored them. Not wanting to be noticed by them—or anyone—she quietly moved through the door of the staff room and sat on the sofa. The room spun, and her mouth felt dry, like she had been without a drink for hours.

Ebony picked up her bag from the floor and fumbled through the pockets, looking for her tablets. She pulled out empty packet after empty packet, and Ebony's heart started to thump against her chest. Panic started to build. If she didn't have any tablets then she didn't have a clue what she would do. She couldn't afford to pass out—hell, she couldn't afford to spend any longer in the staff room. Barney would soon come looking for her.

The crinkle of a packet against her palm as she dug into the bottom of her bag gave her hope, which soared when she found just two tablets left. Despite the foul taste, she threw both into her mouth and swallowed. Shuddering at the aftertaste, Ebony instantly felt the wooziness reduce.

"Thank fuck for that," she whispered, and stood, using her hands to steady herself on the arms of the sofa. Ebony took small steps back to the door, determined to look as normal as possible to the customers—and Barney.

As she opened the door, she peeked her head out into

the hall, pleased to see that the women and man had gone. A sense of relief flowed through her as she walked down the hallway. Ebony had felt that something wasn't quite normal with the women, and she didn't want any part of it. Too mixed up in her own thoughts, Ebony didn't hear the footsteps from behind. Didn't realise she was in danger. Not until she felt an arm slide around her neck and the sharp point of a knife at her ribs.

"Shhhh, don't scream now, Princess. We don't want anyone to hear you."

This time, Ebony's heart trebled its beat in her ribcage. Fear had her mouth fusing shut as she shook her head.

"Good girl." The foul breath of her attacker filled her nostrils, and she had to force back her gag reflex that wanted to take over. The overwhelming stench of rotting meat had seared its way into her senses.

"Come, let's go somewhere more private," he almost purred in her ear, bringing an answering shudder of repulsion that tore through her. *Is this the end?* Ebony thought, over and over again in her mind. Ripped away from the world and forgotten, as if she had never existed. There wouldn't even be anyone to miss her.

The pain of the knife digging into her had her moving at the same pace of the male that held her in a vice-like grip. His fingers wrapped around her braid where it hung over her shoulder. Without somehow attracting any attention, they had made it out of the back door and into the dark alley. The sounds of a busy London could be heard as life went on around her, unaware of the fear and panic she was going through.

Ebony had always thought of herself as a strong person. She had the ability to shrug off the shit that happened to her and carry on regardless. Only this time, the *shit* had

become too much. She was drowning from the onslaught, and she had no way out. No way to breathe. No hope of survival.

Closing her eyes, she finally found her voice, "Please."

"Please what, Princess? Don't kill you? Oh, I wish it were that simple, but my boss wants your head." His words travelled through her, making her breath hitch as tears slid down her face. The pressure of the knife increased, and she felt the tip slice through her skin.

"Remember now, no screaming." He laughed and sniffed her hair. "Although, I am tempted to try the goods before I kill you."

Ebony felt the pressure of the knife reduce as his words penetrated her skull. She had never been a wimp, and the thought of someone touching her like that gave her the little bit of strength she needed. She threw her head back, hitting her attacker in the face. His arm released her neck and braid, and she made to move forward, wanting out of his arms.

Pain like nothing she had ever known hit her, but she kept going. Needing to get space between her and her potential killer.

"Bitch!" he spat out from behind her. "You will pay for that." She felt his hand grab at her braid, the length now flush against her back, and he tugged hard, pulling her head back and throwing her to the unforgiving concrete.

Ebony's fear and panic now controlled her. Fear from the pain of dying, and panic... panic from never living the life she had wanted to. From always letting the negatives stop her from being happy, and from never finding love.

Tears fell as she watched the man step over her prone form. She had no strength. She had never had any strength. Lack of food and medication meant she was always weak and tired, and

what energy she did have had been used up in her futile attempt to escape. The eyes of the man bored into her. They were dark and filled with malice. An unknown hatred that fired his rage.

"You know what?" He sneered as he pressed a knee into her stomach. He knelt closer, the knife now pressed to her chest. "Go on," he began, and pressed again, the knife edge slicing through the flesh above her heart, like the proverbial knife through butter, "scream for me, Princess."

He continued to add pressure, and Ebony knew, right then and there, this was it.

So she screamed—screamed with everything she had, until her ears rang and her breath stopped. Until oblivion took her.

～

Nathan's booted feet slammed against the concrete as he ran towards the scream. It had only lasted mere seconds, but it had called to every single one of his protective instincts. As a nightwalker man, females were to be protected. But as a nightwalker elite guardsman, they protected all that were preyed on. Diving down the alley, he could see the outline of a hooded man as he knelt over a prone figure. Nathan could smell the blood in the air. His daggers were already palmed, and he let one fly. He'd aimed to incapacitate the male, not kill.

The blow hit true, knocking the male off the prone female—the barmaid—although the knife he had been using was still lodged within her.

The male bounced to his feet and faced off with Nathan. Dripping fangs and a slightly elongated face gave his origin away.

"Thought I could smell wet dog," Nathan sneered, and stalked the werewolf, manoeuvring his body so he was in front of the female.

"Fucking nightwalker," the <u>were</u> sneered. "Always putting their noses in where they ain't wanted." He watched as the *were* ripped the dagger free from the back of his shoulder and threw it to the ground.

"Tell me, what does your kind want with a mortal?" Nathan asked. Werewolves were never the ones behind any attack. Their race had fallen far from the days of old. They were now simply hired thugs, paid to do the dirty jobs the wealthy refused.

"As if I'm going to tell a nightwalker guard," the male snorted. He moved slightly to the left, bouncing on the balls of his feet. "Just goes to show you nightwalkers ain't all-powerful and all-knowing."

Nathan gripped his second dagger lightly and waited. He was a patient man, but his nose could only stand the stench of the dog for so long. Tracking the male, he watched, then let the dagger fly as the male bounced to the left. The dagger pierced flesh, right to the hilt, and in the time it took the *were* to realise he had been hit, Nathan was on him. He wrapped a hand around his throat, and lifted. The <u>were</u> was large, but not as big as Nathan—an advantage he used to the max.

"Tell me who sent you after a mortal," he ordered. His own fangs lengthened and pushed against his lower lip. He would never drink from a <u>were,</u> but he wasn't opposed to using them as a scare tactic.

"Talk," he growled.

"Why should I?" the *were* choked out. "You going to let me live if I do?"

Nathan squeezed a little tighter. "I may make your passing a little less painful."

"Fuck you."

Nathan growled louder, his fingers digging in to the male's neck.

"Pathetic, nightwalker. I'm dead anyway if I don't kill the princess. Go. To. Hell."

The _were_ laughed, and Nathan squeezed again. This time the alley echoed with the snap of the _were's_ neck. He dropped him to the floor and turned to the mortal. What did he mean by princess? There was only two, and he had got them to safety.

Nathan knelt next to the female and gently took the knife in his hand. Luckily for her, the _were_ had placed it incorrectly. The blade had only penetrated as far as her sternum would allow. Removing it, Nathan placed a hand over her heart and smiled slightly as he felt the weak pulse there. Like his sister, he had a small amount of healing power. It was weak, but it would allow the bleeding to stop. She would need a lot more attention from Rema, but for now, she was as stable as he could get her. The smell of her blood did nothing to fire his bloodlust, yet it called to him on another level. Urged him closer.

He had completely ignored her in the bar when he had fetched the girls, but now he knew she was in no immediate danger, he took his time. A beautiful face—even with her eyes closed, it was obvious. Her nose small and dainty, and lips that should look out of place on her face, but didn't. Their plumpness called to him, brought to him thoughts of tasting their ripeness until they became swollen from his ministrations.

Nathan shook his head. Thoughts like this, for him, were rare, and very much out of character. Yet it felt natural. His

fingers, of their own accord, moved to stroke the skin on her jaw, relishing in the softness that he found— a pleasant contrast to his own callused hand. In his simple action, her head fell to the side, revealing a birthmark behind her right ear. A crescent moon.

One that matched the two women he had guarded for twenty-two years.

A mark that identified her as the third daughter of Queen Angelica. He pulled his hand away and stared at the female in front of him. Features he hadn't picked up on before now stood out.

The *were* had been right: she was a princess. One he had left twenty-two years before, thinking she was dead.

She was far from it.

6

NATHAN GENTLY PICKED up the unconscious form of the female, careful not to jostle her too much. The wound on her chest had stopped bleeding, but only just. He hadn't missed the dark shadows under her eyes, nor the sickly pale colour of her skin.

Questions—why and how—flew through his head, but right now they were not important. He had to get her to safety, and he had to do it fast. If the *were* had been sent to kill her, there was no telling how many others had received the same order.

He cradled her slight form in his arms and moved away from *The Back Door*. Ironic that the lost princess had been found working in an immortal bar. Especially when he didn't think she knew who and what she actually was.

Voices, closer than he expected, echoed off the brickwork. Nathan quickened his pace, and dived into a shadowed doorway just as the owners of the voices appeared. Keeping his back to the alley, Nathan pressed the princess into the corner, hiding her from view. He closed his eyes, drawing on a small amount of power. As a nightwalker, he

had—like all of his kind—certain gifts. He pulled on the shadows, closing them in around him, distorting his shape in the hopes that whoever the newcomers were, would walk right by. He trusted no one after the attack—no one but his own guard. But his guard were not close by, and signalling them would attract more attention than he wanted. He needed to get the princess back to the mansion as soon as possible.

"Bash," a loud voice sounded, too close for Nathans comfort. Every muscle tensed, ready. He reached out with his senses, picking up the changes in the air, the different smells.

"Yeah," another voice chimed back. Its gravelly tone caused the hairs on Nathan's neck to prick in warning. Another *were, and* as he had just found, a dangerous foe. One that, although he was hidden from sight, may still detect Nathan by smell.

"Where is she?" the voice growled out. Nathan tilted his head as his skin reacted to the power that now flowed through the air. Warlock. Nathan sneered. He hated warlocks. Most of the immortal races did. It was why his queen had gone into hiding to have her children. Hybrids— or the idea of creating one—was considered abhorrent, a being that should never be allowed to exist. Only now, thanks to the queen's stubbornness, three females, both nightwalker and Wiccan, existed—much to the dislike of the very council that had threatened to end them. Only now they saw them as a chance to gain control over the other races.

"She—she," the *were* stuttered, his voice filled with fear. Nathan, in any other situation, would have snorted. *Weres* used to be a proud and loyal race, afraid of little. It was a pity to see how far they had fallen.

"Oh, spit it out. I haven't got all fucking day," the warlock sneered. Nathan tracked his movements—the heels on his shoes smacked against the cement as he paced. He had a feeling he was circling the *were*, his power reaching out in a bid to terrify.

"She..." He stalled again. "A nightwalker."

"What!" the warlock erupted, his power shooting out, hitting Nathan in the back. He held in his grunt of pain. Every nerve ending felt like it was on fire, and he shook from the strain of holding up the princess and keeping his own power around him.

The *were* whimpered. This time the sound came from further down the alley, and the smell of blood filled the air.

"You let a nightwalker get to her first?" The words of the warlock vibrated with anger, "You let her not only live, but fall into the hands of our enemy?

An enemy that, once they realise what they have, could cause more trouble than your little canine mind could compre-fucking-hend."

"Oscar had her," the *were* pleaded. "It was Oscar's fault."

"And now your friend is dead, and a nightwalker has our quarry," the warlock sneered.

"I'm sorry," the *were* whispered, almost beyond Nathan's ability to hear.

"Clifford... Please. I'm sorry."

The *were's* voice rose higher in pitch as his fear took over. Nathan could picture the mongrel curled on the ground, begging for his life.

"Enough," the warlock named Clifford shouted. "You have disappointed me, and for that, I should really snap your neck like the nightwalker did to Oscar."

"No! Please."

"Imagine what our leader will say when I tell him you

have lost her."

Only whimpers could be heard.

"But I will forgive you."

Nathan pulled the female closer into his body. Sweat coated his brow. "Come on, fucking move, will you," his whispered under his breath.

"You will?" the **were** asked.

"Yes, I will. Go. Leave me." The sound of feet on concrete could be heard as the *were* did as he was told, scuttling off as fast as his feet could carry him. Nathan still didn't move. He didn't trust warlocks—hell, he didn't trust any of the other races.

"Come out, come out, nightwalker, and give me back my prize."

"Shit," Nathan whispered. The warlock had simply been waiting, and now he had Nathan cornered.

"Don't make me wait, Nightwalker," the Warlock called out. "I don't like being made to wait."

Nathan had a choice to make. Either stay hidden for as long as he could hold the shadows—though he wasn't the strongest when it came to his powers. He was more a fighter than anything else—or, he could show himself and hope that he could talk himself and the princess out of this mess.

Sweat had started to drip down his face. There was no way he would be able to hold his position for much longer. Nathan had made his choice: he would face the warlock. If that meant he would be in a fight for his life, then so be it. He had taken an oath to protect those with Queen Angelica's blood, and he took his oaths seriously.

Hoisting the still unconscious female into his arms, he released his power, letting the shadows drop and revealing his position in the doorway. Nathan turned and walked out to face the male warlock.

"Ahh, not just any nightwalker—the big man himself." He grinned. His greasy, dark hair was loose and fell across his brow. With a sweep of his hand, he bowed. "I am Clifford, and you are Nathaniel, Captain of the Elite Guard."

Nathan nodded, but said nothing—there wasn't anything to say.

"Not talking, huh?" The warlock shrugged. "You nightwalkers were always on the quiet side." He stepped closer. Nathan's only reaction was gripping the female tighter to him.

"Give me the female," the warlock said, his voice calm and quiet, yet the hairs on the back of Nathan's scalp prickled as he felt the warlock's power build.

"No," he answered, and allowed his fangs to elongate, pushing over his lower lip.

"Ooh, scary vampire." The warlock laughed and raised his hand. Instantly, Nathan felt an invisible hand wrap around his throat, cutting off his air supply. The phantom grip tightened with each passing second.

Nathan growled, even as the air into his lungs halted. His eyes narrowed, never leaving the smirking face of the warlock. His sight became fuzzy around the edges. Unconsciousness threatened to take over, but Nathan fought it with everything he had.

Nathan's eyes closed as his body took the strain. The phantom grip tightened further. His lungs burned from the lack of oxygen, and the darkness closed in on him.

So much for putting up a fight. He had once again let not only himself down, but the female in his arms. He had let down his race. But what could he do? He had no magic like the warlock. He had only his daggers and his fists.

His daggers.

Straining, Nathan moved his right hand, his body

shaking from the lack of oxygen and holding the female against him. Nathan forced his eyes open again. As much as his vision was dimming, he could still see the warlock's smug grin.

"Aww, look at the nightwalker fight." His condescending tone pissed Nathan off.

Anger coursed through him, and he let it. His hand found his dagger, and he took hold, drawing it out from under his jacket.

"Oh look, he's got a—" The warlock's voice cut off and was instead replaced with a cry of pain, followed by a gargle. The pressure on Nathan's throat eased instantly, and he dropped to one knee. Oxygen burst into his deprived lungs, filling them.

His gaze still fuzzy, Nathan looked at the warlock. His body laid face-up on the floor, his eyes open and his body fitting.

"Stupid warlocks," a chirpy voice sounded from beyond the warlock's form. "They always have to fart-arse about." A male, similar in height to himself, stood holding a small box in his hand and a stupid grin on his face. His blonde hair fell in luxurious waves around him, and his green eyes sparkled with mischief. "Man, I've always wanted to play with a taser," he said, laughing as he toed the now unconscious form of the warlock.

"I love the way he just twitches every now and again, and at the same time, pisses himself." The newcomer grinned and stepped over the body. Walking a few steps further, he bent down in front of Nathan.

"Sorry I'm late, but Ivory wouldn't shut up and, well, you know how she is." He shrugged, and then continued, introducing himself,

"I'm Gale. I'm the cavalry."

Nathan made to answer when the female in his arms suddenly moved. Her own arms started to flail, and a scream ripped from her lungs and filled the alley. Its echo bounced off the brickwork.

Her flailing arms smacked into Nathan's face at the same time her legs sent Gale to his arse.

"Shhhhh, it's ok," Nathan's husky voice cooed in an attempt to calm her, but one look at her fear-filled grey eyes and he knew she was too lost to memory.

"Calm," he said sternly, hoping that approach would work, but there was still no change—in fact, she struggled harder.

His fangs had yet to recede, and that only helped to make things worse.

"Here, let me," Gale offered. Nathan was unable to stop the growl as it fell from his throat. It was unexpected—to both of them.

"I'm an imp. I can send her to sleep. It's not gonna hurt her," Gale said, raising a blonde eyebrow.

"I promise."

Nathan looked down at the female and nodded.

"Do it."

He growled out, knowing this was the only way they could get her safely back to the mansion.

The imp placed a palm upon the female's forehead and closed his eyes. Moments later, she calmed. Her hands ceased their movements and she quickly fell into a deep sleep. Her body relaxed in to Nathan's and, surprisingly, Nathan loved it.

The feel of her nestled in his embrace was perfect and right.

She fit.

It was as simple as that. But it could never be.

7

AT FIRST, Ebony didn't dare open her eyes, not when the last thing she remembered was being surrounded by monsters with bright blue eyes and fangs. She knew they had tried to reason with her, but she had heard little of what they had to say. All she had wanted to do was get away.

She had done what most sane people would have done —she had freaked out.

Both the blonde and the redhead had tried to calm her, even going so far as to restrain her, only Ebony had landed an elbow to the face. Ebony had felt like her heart wanted to burst from her chest as she'd let fear take over. She'd had no clue where she was.

It had taken both females and an unknown male with green eyes to stop her flailing about. The male had touched her forehead, and before she had known what was going on, darkness had once again taken over.

Taking a deep breath, Ebony opened her eyes, but she couldn't focus. A deep sense of panic was still there, but this time she was determined to conquer it and not let it control her—as she had allowed it to do before.

Her memories of the attack filtered through her brain, giving her a blow-by-blow report. It made her heart once again thump against the ribs in her chest. She remembered her attacker and how he had stabbed her with a huge knife. She also recalled watching her short, pathetic life flash before her eyes. Tears trickled down her face, and her chest gave a sympathetic twinge of pain, as if it, too, remembered the feeling of the blade as it cut through flesh.

Bright blue eyes then flashed through her mind, so intense, so filled with heat, she shivered—her memory of them just as potent as the real thing.

Was she dead? Was being warm and rested on a soft surface that enveloped her in comfort what death felt like?

Yes, she had to be dead. She had never been this comfortable in her life—hell, it had been a rare occurrence when she had been warm. Even the usual problems that had plagued her seemed a distance memory.

Yes, she was dead, and by some luck of the draw, they had let her in through the pearly gates. Her eyelids felt like dead weights and had ordered themselves shut again. Ebony had to focus and force them open, only this time she was able to see not the wispy clouds and white light of heaven, but the dark, wooden posts of a bed surrounded on three sides with black, velvet curtains.

Maybe I am in hell then, and they're healing me first, Ebony wondered. Pushing up on her elbows, Ebony took in the bed, and then the room. It was something Ebony had only ever seen online, or in magazines. It was the type of bedroom that belonged to the high-class and wealthy, and she was neither. Lifting her left arm, she felt a tug, before noticing the line that led from her hand up to a bag that looked like it was wrapped in tinfoil.

Whatever was being pumped into her was doing some-

thing no one else had been able to do. It made her feel nearly normal.

"Shit," Ebony blurted, then fought to look at her chest—where she remembered the knife going in.

The pain was like nothing she had ever felt before, a burning that felt like it would overtake her entire body, turning her to ash from the inside. Ebony went to pull the neck of her t-shirt away from her body. It took a moment before she actually noticed that she wasn't in her own clothes. In fact, she wasn't wearing much at all. What she did have on looked expensive, to the point she bet it would have cost more than what she had ever earned in an entire year.

Possibly two.

A stunning dark grey silk nightie covered her body. The thin straps sat lightly on her shoulders. The material coasting across her skin gave her a whole new experience of what wearing an expensive material could feel like.

But who had brought her here? Who had dressed her?

The soft sound of the bedroom door opening had Ebony pulling the duvet right up to her chin. Her eyes watched as a familiar blonde head poked into the room, her bright blue eyes pinning Ebony. The smile that crossed Ivory's face gave Ebony a sinking feeling.

A feeling that her lifesaver she had known it was gone, there was no going back. Whatever had happened had changed it but she still had no idea whether it was for the better or not.

"Ahh, you're awake," Ivory exclaimed, and bolted into the room. Almost childlike, she jumped on the bed and bounced on the end, her grin almost infectious.

"Where am I?" Ebony asked quietly, keeping the duvet

up to her chin. Trust didn't come easily to her. She wanted answers.

"Okay, so don't freak out," Ivory started. "You were attacked, and our guard saved you. Then we brought you here."

Her explanation was far too simple and far too easy. Ebony knew something was off.

"What really happened? And skip the bullshit," she snapped, before adding,

"Who the fuck are you, anyway?"

"Ivory," another female voice called out. This time it was the redhead—Scarlett, she remembered—that walked in. She was nowhere near as bouncy as Ivory, but rather more on the serious side. "Tell her the truth. Tell her everything."

Instead of sitting on the bed, Scarlett walked to the window and sat on the plush cushion that covered the windowsill. There was no light coming through. Ebony then noticed the metal shutters covering the outside.

"Okay," Ivory agreed. "But you have to listen to everything."

Ebony nodded. She would listen—whether she believed them would be another matter.

"Okay. So, do you know who your mother is?" Ivory asked, and all Ebony could do was shake her head. She had been told little of where she came from. All her foster parents had made it clear that they didn't care. On the rare occasions she had plucked up the courage to ask, they had informed her that her mother must have been a druggie, and that she had been left to die.

"What were you told as a child?" Ivory asked, and smiled encouragingly

Ebony shuffled on the bed, feeling uncomfortable at

being watched by the sisters. Their bright blue eyes felt like lasers as they gazed at her.

"I was informed by one of my foster parents that my mother had been a smackhead who had OD'd and left me to die."

Deep in her heart, Ebony had always felt like that was a lie. But what else could have happened? Why would her mother have left her?

"That's simply not true at all." This time it was Scarlett's voice that answered, her tone no longer serious and impatient. Instead, it was quiet and full of emotion.

"Your mother was no smackhead, Ebony. She was beautiful, intelligent, graceful, and just. She loved her people and they loved her. Even now they still bow to her likeness and offer gifts—tokens, in her memory."

"What my sister says is true, Ebony," Ivory agreed with her sister. Ebony looked at them as they gazed back at her, their eyes swimming with emotion and tears.

"How did you know my mother? Who was she?" Ebony asked. Why did these women know more about her own mother than she did?

"Because, Ebony, your mother was Queen of the Night-walkers. A race known to humans as vampyres. She was their ruler," Ivory explained.

"Humans... You say that as if *you* are not human."

"We're not, Ebony, and neither are you." Scarlett had moved from the window seat and approached the bed. Her hand lay gently on her sister's shoulder.

"What? Of course I'm human. I may have issues, but I'm definitely human," Ebony squeaked out. Her mind a complete whirr of questions.

"No, you are not," Ivory answered, and she leaned forward and tapped the IV line that was in the back of

Ebony's hand. "This isn't just saline going into your system." She smiled. "Haven't you noticed how you are feeling ten times better than you were before?"

Ebony looked down at the line, her fingers playing with the plastic. Ivory was correct: she felt amazing compared to how she had felt before.

"What's a nightwalker, and is that the only scary thing out there?" It was the first question Ebony had that fired out of her mouth. It was the only one she felt brave enough to ask.

"Nightwalkers—or vampyres—are an immortal race, Ebony. Don't believe everything you have heard from Hollywood, from the humans mixed-up view on history. It is true that nightwalkers rely on blood to survive. Only, it's the blood of their own race, mainly females that they take. There are many immortal races..." Scarlett started, and Ivory carried on from where she left.

"Warlocks."

"Werewolves."

"Imps."

"Demons. The list could easily go on. Nearly all the immortal races went underground a few centuries ago when humans started to... let's just say, get wise, and began the witch trials."

The information stunned Ebony. All these races that existed and she had no idea. Not one clue—and she could bet she had met a few.

"So, what are you then?" Ebony asked. "What race are you? You never said 'we' when you said nightwalker."

Ivory and Scarlett both grinned, and in doing so, showed their slightly prominent canines.

"Oh, we are nightwalkers, but we are also something

else." Ivory took Ebony's hands in her own. "We are exactly the same as you."

"What?"

"What my bouncy and extremely excited sister is trying to say, is that you, Ebony, are a nightwalker, too, just as we are, and like us, you are also what is called a hybrid."

"A hybrid of what?" Ebony again squeaked out.

"Warlock," Scarlett stated simply.

"How do you know this?"

"Ebony, you weren't abandoned. You were born the third Princess to Queen Angelica, ruler of the nightwalkers. The third prophesised sister born of both blood and magic."

Ebony couldn't breathe, but it was the look in the two women's eyes that had her entranced. A look of hope and happiness.

"Ebony, we've been searching for you for a long time. You are our sister," Ivory whispered, and bent forward on the bed, wrapping Ebony in an embrace that felt not awkward or strange, but more like coming home. Seconds later, a second set of arms cocooned her. Although everything they had said felt like something out of a fantasy film, she believed every word.

She had family.

She wasn't alone anymore. She repeated it over and over in her head.

I'm no longer alone.

NATHAN STOOD QUIETLY by the door and watched the sisters as they finally revealed who they were to Ebony. It would take one cold-hearted bastard to not be affected at all by the reunion. Their voices filled the room. Instead of all three talking over each other, they spoke in sync, taking their turn to tell their story. If anyone doubted that they were related, watching them now would make them a believer.

Nathan hadn't seen Ebony since he had delivered her to her room and made sure she was being taken care of by Rema. Regardless of his own feelings, he was still in charge, and the safety of the girls was now a top priority. Once word was out that the three sisters of prophecy were, in fact, real, he would have the council breathing down his neck, as well as the other races concerned for their own skins.

How Ebony had survived as long as she had, without the protection and care of her own race, amazed Nathan. It showed a strength most never knew they had. Her acceptance of their world—the one she was now a part of—astounded him. For someone that had no clue of the

immortal world, she had taken it all in stride—except for a small episode where she, in short, freaked out.

Now he watched as she sat with her sisters—sat and talked about who she actually was. Who her mother was. The mortals that had found her and then raised her had lied about her mother, stating only that she was the unloved child of a drug addict, which couldn't be further from the truth. The emotions that crossed Ebony's face ranged from hope to complete relief, before she found herself engulfed within the arms of both Ivory and Scarlett. Tears fell freely from all three of the females, causing an answering ache within Nathan's own gut.

He couldn't imagine what it must feel like to have known nothing about your family, only to find them, out of the blue. To find out you are worth so much more than what people had told you. Guilt ate at Nathan—guilt that he had left not only his queen's body, but also Ebony's. Rema had been positive that the child had been stillborn, yet here she was.

A survivor.

A fighter. More like the queen than Ivory or Scarlett.

Now that all three were together, he could see how similar they were. All were hauntingly beautiful, with wide eyes, full lips, and high cheekbones. Ebony still looked thinner than her sisters, but the more she fed, the more she would heal. All three had long hair that reached the centre of their backs. Yet, the each embraced their own unique qualities.

Ivory, with her long blonde hair, had always been the bouncy, almost erratic sister, who spent a great deal of time chatting to anyone and everyone, as well as annoying his second-in-command. Nathan knew there was more to that then either of them let on, but it was not his business.

Scarlett, with her long red hair, was not what you would expect of a redhead. She was quieter and more reserved, yet she had a power few knew of. To the outside world, they were the spoilt offspring of a long-dead queen. Only those that had watched them as they had grown knew there was nothing farther from the truth.

They had powers the council knew nothing about—powers that originated from their warlock father. Powers that, if the other immortal fractions found out about before the girls were ready, could cause outright war. He looked upon both Ivory and Scarlett as his charges—watched them grow into the women they were now. His feelings for them were ones of a protective nature, so the feelings that were surging to the forefront now, for the third sister, were out of place.

From the moment he had seen Ebony in that alley, feelings he had not known before had assaulted him, and now here he stood, skulking in the shadows, watching her. Being the beast that the mortals thought they were. She was, to him, more beautiful than her sisters. Her long, dark hair shone in the dim light of the room. Its waves caressed her skin and made his fingers clench with the need to sweep it off her shoulders. Her eyes, still a light grey, had yet to change to the blue that identified her as a nightwalker. A part of him wanted them to stay as they were—they were filled with every emotion that filtered across her face. In all his existence, he had done his duty, protected his queen and his race. Now, he had to fight against every instinct he had to stop himself scooping Ebony into his arms and leaving with her. Protecting only her and no one else. In the irrational part of his mind, she was all that mattered.

What was wrong with him?

Nathan, so distracted with his inner thoughts, missed

their conversation, until one word alerted his attention, and held it: feeding.

He listened, and with each word, his muscles grew taught, his fangs elongated, and his chest heaved.

Ebony's voice was soft as she asked her questions,

"When you say feed, what exactly do you mean?"

Nathan's jaw tightened as a mental image of Ebony's neck exposed to him burst into his mind's eye.

"Okay," Ivory started. "So, as nightwalkers, we have to feed, but because we are hybrids—or special, as I like to say—we can also survive on real food." Ivory laughed. "As you have found out, though, through personal experience, the lack of feeding means other issues can occur."

"By feeding, I'm assuming you mean blood?" Ebony asked again. Nathan growled under his breath. Ivory had an annoying way of explaining things yet not answering the damn question.

"Yes. In a way, we have the best of both worlds. We have to drink blood," Ivory shrugged as Scarlett glared at her for being direct, "but we can also indulge in chocolate cake, too".

Ebony nodded, but her attention had turned to the silver bag that was hooked to her IV line. Gently, she poked it, and winced as she heard the sloshing of blood as it hit the side of the bag. Most safe houses of the nightwalkers had a supply of bagged blood for any emergencies when a donor couldn't be found. But for Ebony to truly heal, she would need her next feed to be direct from the source. A morsel of information the sisters had yet to drop into the conversation.

Scarlett, this time, stepped forward, taking over from her sister. Nathan smiled. It seemed he wasn't the only one getting annoyed with Ivory's ramblings.

Scarlett's husky voice filled the room as she spoke, "You

know all those movies you've seen where the vamp takes off with a victim and drains them dry?" Scarlett waited for Ebony to nod. "Well, it's nothing like that."

"Nightwalkers have to feed from another of their race. Ideally of the opposite sex. You still following?"

Ebony nodded again. This time, though, she looked worried. She was gently chewing her lip and twisting the duvet in her hands.

A giggle from Ivory had Nathan glaring at the back of her head.

"Usually a feeding is more than just that. It can... err..." Scarlett blushed, and Ivory dove right in to continue,

"It can become rather hot and heavy," she said, emphasising the 'hot and heavy' with her fingers.

"Oh?"

"Yeah," Ivory grinned, her voice almost a purr.

"Very hot," she said, as a dreamy expression crossed her face.

"So, you both have boyfriends to feed from?" Ebony asked.

Nathan's fists clenched again, the knuckles cracking. He had to force himself to take a deep breath. Nightwalkers didn't do the normal boyfriend/girlfriend relationships that mortals rely on. No, a relationship for a nightwalker was for life. A mating that merged their souls into one. So, the feeding would only really occur between mates. Usually. But not always.

"We don't have boyfriends, honey," Scarlett started. "I have Angus, who is one of the Elite Guard. He is also gay, so we are both safe from any amorous feelings." Scarlett smiled this time. "He's also as close to a brother as I can get."

"What about you, Ivory?"

"Ivory is in denial. Bishop, also a member of the Elite Guard, is her donor."

"But not your boyfriend?"

"Nope. Honey, we have mates, not boyfriends," Ivory continued. "Only Bishop... Well, with him, it's complicated."

Nathan smirked at seeing the usually unflappable Ivory blushing at the thought of his second-in-command. Ivory had been messing with him for a while now, and Bishop was at the end of his tether. Nathan had seen the strain. It wouldn't surprise him at all to find out that Bishop had finally claimed the blonde sister, sooner rather than later.

"So, what will I do?" Ebony asked. The words barely penetrated his mind. Any answer the sisters had given were drowned out by an intense buzzing in his head. His feet moved, and he had little physical awareness to control them.

In seconds, he had moved into the room. He ignored the other sisters. Instead, his gaze sought, found, and pinned Ebony.

Words erupted from his mouth, ones he had no control over, and for once, he didn't care.

"I will feed you—anytime you need," he growled. "No one else."

Ebony listened to everything her new-found sisters had said. She had two choices:

One, accept the truth—every single detail. Or secondly, realise that she had finally lost the plot and would need to be signed up for that famous white jacket.

Only, she had this strange, tingly gut-feeling she wasn't crazy. So she had asked questions and attempted to take it all in. A part of her wanted to freak out once again—maybe

run around the room screaming, or just hide under the duvet—but she had a feeling the two stunners sat on her bed wouldn't let her do that.

When she tried to think about what they had said, only one or two random words seemed to stand out. Immortal. Queen. Vampyres.

"Feeding," Ebony repeated. Her mind wandered through scenes of movies she had seen—scenes that depicted blood and death, as well as quite a bit of throat ripping. She couldn't suppress the shudder that cascaded through her body.

Her sisters either ignored the shudder or didn't notice as they took her single word for a question, diving into a full explanation of what and how. According to Ivory, it was a pleasurable and intense experience—only her face told her it was a damn sight more than that. The blonde's eyes became all dreamy as she was lost to memory. Whoever the male was, this Bishop meant more to her than she would let on.

"So, what will I do?" Ebony blurted out, not sure where the question had come from. But she was intrigued to know what they had planned. The whole idea of drinking some-one's blood actually made her stomach turn. Add to that the fact she didn't have fangs like Ivory or scarlet, and she felt at a disadvantage.

Ivory looked at her sister and opened her mouth, only nothing came out. The sound that filled the room consisted of a low growl, and was followed by the slamming of the bedroom door against the wood. There, in the open door-way, stood a man so huge, his head nearly hit the lintel. His stride as he stalked into the room made the distance between the bed and door vanish. Only his bright blue eyes, similar to those of Ivory and Scarlett, made her frown. A

familiarity hit her, and once again, memories from her attack fought to take over, only this time she didn't feel herself sliding into a panic attack. This time she wasn't afraid... because of this man.

His presence charged the atmosphere, making it feel heavy and difficult to take a deep breath.

The words that were grunted out through clenched, fanged teeth made her heart stop, then start again, this time at double the speed.

His eyes bored into her, the bright blue holding her in their intensity. "I will feed you—anytime you need." He growled again. "No one else."

Ebony's brain struggled to fire on all cylinders as the original notion of movie vampyres sucking the life from their victims was replaced with the image of this male's body hard and heavy against her own, his breath on her neck, before the slow slide of fang on flesh. She no longer felt repulsed, and her body fought against the need to climb out of the covers and give herself to this male. She felt on the verge of combustion from his gaze alone. Afraid of what she might do, Ebony moved slightly to the side, hiding her face behind Ivory's back, letting her new sister take the lead in a situation that Ebony had zero idea about how to deal with.

The blonde's voice was laced with sarcasm, the distraction giving Ebony time to get herself under control.

"Nathan... Hi. thank you so much for knocking."

Ebony watched him from under her lashes. His eyes still hadn't left her, despite her hidden position. His slight wince wasn't missed, and she couldn't stop the slight smile that graced her lips. Now that she could see him while no attack was happening, or being under duress, she was impressed. Not only was he huge in height and width, but he was

gorgeous. With hair that reached his collar and lips that should be illegal on a man, he was her type—and then some.

"What do you mean you will feed her?" The pitch of Ivory's voice gradually got higher. "I don't think that's your decision to make."

Scarlett chimed in. Both sisters seemed, instead of thankful for the offer, pissed. Pissed enough that Scarlett's eyes had started to glow.

E bony didn't know what that meant, but she was certain it wasn't good, especially with the way Scarlett's fingers were circling. She was no expert, but she had seen *Harry Potter*. Ignoring the call of Ivory, Ebony threw back the covers and bounded out of bed. She ignored the sting as the IV line was pulled free from her skin.

As quick as she could, she was stood in front of the male named Nathan. She didn't want him hurt. She didn't know him, yet she knew she couldn't watch her sister hurt him.

"Stop, Scarlett, please," she called out. "I don't know what mumbo jumbo you ladies can do, but this guy saved me, and is offering to feed me, which, to me, is kind. After all, he doesn't even know me and he's offering his blood," Ebony argued, and from her new position, she could see that Ivory's eyes had indeed also started to glow.

"Did you know your eyes glowed?" she asked, totally off topic. "Is that normal?"

Large hands cupped her bare shoulders, and her body reacted instantaneously. Heat erupted from his touch and fanned out across her body. The ability to think, let alone talk, fled, and all she could do was bask in that heat.

"Ebony," a voice whispered across her ear, causing an answering shiver, "I will leave now, but I will return tonight so you can feed."

Nathan's voice was strong yet quiet, and she could have sworn she felt lips press to the side of her head. She nodded in response. Her head had barely completed the action when the heat, and his presence, was gone, leaving her cold in its wake.

"Ebony, are you listening to us?"

Ebony shook her head and wrapped her arms around her waist.

"No, sorry. What did you say?" Ivory and Scarlett grinned.

"What?" she asked again.

"You were wrong, you know," Scarlett said, and Ebony frowned.

"About what?"

Silently, both sisters guided Ebony over to the gilded, full-length mirror that sat in the corner of the room.

Her reflection peered back at her, only she looked different, and couldn't quite tell why.

"Wrong about what?" she repeated.

Both sisters peered over her shoulders. Each one took her hand. In the mirror, all three stood, finally united. One blonde, one red, and one raven.

"You do have fangs. Look..." Ivory breathed.

"Welcome home, Ebony," Scarlett whispered.

THE FIRE CRACKLED and snapped from the large, ornate fire-place. The wood of the surround, darkened with age, drew in the light from the fire, which then reflected off its shiny, polished surface, causing the shadows to dance in the recesses of the old ballroom.

The once decadent room had decayed over time. What was once a place of laughter, light, and dance, now held only darkness.

That was how Gregori liked it.

The red and gold from the flickering fire cast its gaze over the bent form of the self-made king. On his knees, he bowed, arms spread wide, until his forehead touched the floor, where the light flickered again over the pentagram that had been rendered. The liquid that had been used to draw it shifted from a bright red to a dull black.

At first glance, he was an ordinary man, whose looks could entice even the most cold-hearted of women. Yet once in his company, they would soon sense something was not quite right, and that fight or flight instinct would kick in. Only then, it would be too late.

With long brown hair that fell in waves past his broad shoulders, and almost golden-brown eyes, he wasn't easily forgotten. Power radiated from him, making an almost visible aura, yet it was—as the room—tainted with darkness.

As a warlock, he had access to the energies of the earth, yet that had never been enough. The darkness had offered him more, and he had taken it with both hands and submerged himself in a long-forgotten art.

"My lord," a quiet voice whispered, its tone echoing through the room.

Gregori gave no answer. He kept his head bent and mind on the task at hand.

"My lord," the voice called again, this time louder, only to be cut off with a gurgle as Gregori's hand shot out. The warlock silently rose to his feet, straightening to his full height of well over six feet.

"How dare you interrupt me," his deep voice growled as he turned and faced the two men that had entered the room. His eyes that were usually brown now radiated with a golden glow as power vibrated through him.

"I... I..."

"Silence!" he snapped. His hand pointed to the pentagram. "Can you not see I was busy?"

Gregori glared at the two males before he turned and stalked towards a raised platform on which a large wooden chair sat. The grace of his movements as he lowered himself into it belied his large frame.

"So, what is it that's so important you had the nerve to interrupt me?" he asked, and watched as the two males stepped forward.

"My lord... we come with—"

"If you say *bad news*, I will string you up by your balls."

The male cowered, shifting into a submissive posture, which made Gregori grin. So much for the pride of **weres**. This one had been easy to train.

"My lord, if I may..." The other male—a warlock, though his powers were weak—stepped forward. He kept his chin held high.

"I will admit we failed, but we encountered an issue—well, two."

"Tell me." Gregori inclined his head as a signal to continue and rested his chin in his palm. Regardless of their excuses, he was not happy, and failure would not be tolerated.

"My lord, the female was located, yet when the **were**, Oscar, went to finish the job, he was set upon by none other than Nathaniel."

"What!" Gregori roared. "You let a fucking nightwalker take her?"

Gregori stood, and instead of firing his anger at the warlock, he let it loose upon the **were**. He reached out with a hand. The **were** screamed and contorted as he was lifted into the air. Smoke rose from his skin, and the smell of searing flesh filled the great room. Gregori grinned, his eyes once again glowing a bright gold as he accepted the darkness and its power.

The **were** continued to scream, even as he was pushed against the wall of the ballroom, his body almost melting into the plaster. There, Gregori fused the **were** to the wall, still alive but now unable to move.

Gregori turned and faced the now kneeling warlock. Clifford had been one of the few he had trusted to get a job done, but with knowledge of the latest report, he now doubted his usefulness and loyalty. Fear radiated from him, and he loved it. This was what it was to have power. To instil

such fear in a man... it was almost as addictive as the power that coursed through him.

"Tell me, do you know where they have taken the girl?"

"No, my lord," Clifford answered. "But we *will* find her and kill her, as instructed. We will not fail you again."

"Do not make promises you cannot keep," Gregori warned, his tone exposing the underlying threat. He sat back on his throne and admired his latest piece of art. The **were** thrashed around in pain from his position on the wall, yet he was still trying to strategically shift his body in an effort to free himself.

"But—" Clifford responded, but was silenced with a glare from Gregori.

"Leave me. I suggest you use every resource to track down the location of the female, or else you, too, will be gracing my walls."

"Yes, my lord," Clifford breathed, fear and relief filling his words. He climbed to his feet, keeping a bowed posture until he had left the hall.

"Are you sure that's wise?" a new voice asked. This one wasn't filled with fear, but genuine curiosity.

"Justin." Gregori nodded to the male as he appeared from a shadowed entrance. "What news do you bring me?" he asked, ignoring the warlock's question.

"All three females are reunited, as you suspected. Getting to them won't be easy," he answered. "Did you really have to send Clifford on a fool's errand when you already know the answer?" he asked again

"Clifford is a means to an end. Sending him out will keep him out of the way. For now," Gregori replied.

He tapped a finger against his chin as he absorbed the latest news. That the sisters had reunited had him intrigued.

"I have had a change of heart, Justin. The females... I want to meet them," he calmly stated.

"Make it so."

"Yes, my lord," Justin said, and bowed before he vanished back into the shadows.

Gregori watched the flames of the fire, lost in thought. The females were hybrids—half warlock, half nightwalker. That in itself was an abomination, and one he would personally rid the world of, but only in the right way. Sending a **were** had been somewhat hasty on his part, and as he thought about it even more, he realised he needed to create a better plan.

He couldn't allow the females the time to grow and learn the power that was in their blood—blood that also ran through his veins.

Gregori craved power more than life itself. Even if it meant destroying the life of his own daughters.

Ebony once again found herself looking up at the canopy that covered the bed. Only this time, she wasn't freaked out, or scared, or even confused. She had spent most of the night talking to Ivory and Scarlett about what and who she actually was.

It was still a lot to take in, but she would take it one day at a time. Only, she still couldn't help but feel like she was trapped in a dream, that at any moment she would wake up on the dingy couch in the staff room of the bar.

Ebony smiled and stretched her hands over her head. She felt... good. The drip, the line of which had been reinserted after Nathan's departure, had been removed whilst she had been asleep, and she no longer felt the twinge of exhaustion that had plagued her most of her life. Even in the darkened room she could see perfectly, and, for once, her eyes no longer hurt.

All this was due to the transplant she had received, but —and she was quoting Ivory—*if she didn't neck someone soon, her new-found health would once again deteriorate.*

The mere thought of 'necking someone', Ebony still

found a little gross. The idea of swallowing someone's blood just didn't sit right, but she knew—after Scarlett had shouted at her—that it needed to be done. At least she didn't have to worry about finding someone—that choice had been made for her when the gorgeous and grumpy Nathan had offered.

Well, not offered, more like demanded that he be the one to feed her. On a level, it scared her to share that sort of intimacy with someone she hardly knew, yet she couldn't bring herself to turn him down. He had been the one to save her life, and maybe he felt some obligation to her—to make sure she was fully healed before he palmed her off on someone else.

Whatever it was, she would go through with it, but only so she could heal fully. Although, she still had no idea what that meant.

"Ebony, child, you are awake," a lyrical voice called from the doorway. She turned her head to see an older woman enter the room, a tray in her arms.

"Rema?" Ebony questioned, not sure if the woman that had been coming and going in her dreams had been real or a figment of her wappy imagination.

"Yes, dear. I'm so glad you are ok," Rema answered as she placed the tray on the bedside table. "To see you here after all these years fills my heart with joy."

The lady smiled and took Ebony's hands in her own, before kissing them. Ebony watched as tears left her bright blue eyes.

"I am so, so sorry."

"What for? You have been nothing but kind to me since I arrived," Ebony asked, unsure what she could possibly be sorry for. They had only known each other a day and a half. Definitely not enough time to do anything.

"Oh, sweet child... I was there—the day you were born," Rema started, and Ebony felt her heart thump against her chest.

"We thought you were stillborn. You were blue and showed no sign of life." Rema's tears came fast now, the sobs giving her hiccups.

"We placed you into your mother's arms. We had to leave as dawn was approaching... We didn't know, Ebony... Oh, I am so, so sorry."

Rema's sobs erupted into tears of anguish and sorrow that pulled at Ebony's heartstrings. She didn't blame anyone for her abandonment, and even now that she knew the truth, she just felt contented. A part of her felt happy that she had, in fact, been wanted, that it was bad luck that had pulled her away from her family.

"Rema..." she started, and tugged on her hands, gaining her attention, "I don't blame you or anyone else. Please, it's ok," she cooed, yet Rema continued to sob.

"Rema," she called again, and this time was rewarded with bright blue eyes looking up at her. "It wasn't your fault," Ebony stated slowly, making sure Rema took in every word.

"You don't...?" she asked between sobs.

"No. I've never blamed anyone. There was no one to blame," Ebony admitted, and gave a weak smile. "I was just in a shitty situation, and I was trying my best to get out of it."

"Oh, child!" Rema wrapped Ebony in a hug that, again, should have felt awkward, but instead, it gave her a sense of coming home.

"Okay, enough of my wailing." Rema laughed quietly. She released Ebony and pulled a small handkerchief from her pocket with which she wiped her eyes. Ebony said

nothing and pretended to straighten the duvet, so she had more time to calm herself.

"Right, it's nearly nightfall, so I will be heading out to get some shopping. Your sisters somehow manage to put away an obscene amount of food." She laughed as she shrugged. "Now you are on the mend, is there anything you would like?" Rema asked, and this time, her smile was wide, the tears all but gone.

Ebony couldn't help but return the smile as she pulled the covers back and climbed out of bed.

"Tea—definitely tea, and maybe chocolate cake." She smiled but lowered her head in slight embarrassment. "I haven't had chocolate cake since I was five," Ebony admitted.

"Chocolate cake it is, my dear." Rema cupped Ebony's face and beamed at her. "Welcome home. You are so like your mother."

With that said, she patted her cheek then left the room, leaving Ebony now on the verge of tears.

Her mind was still processing the shock of finding out that not only were beings of myth a reality, but that she was, in fact, one of them. She had spent a good hour, before she had drifted off, touching her teeth, until her new fangs had receded.

Her sleep had been plagued by dreams of penetrating eyes, a large body, and fangs, which, surprisingly, hadn't scared her. Instead, they had caused butterflies to erupt every time she thought of the one person she knew that had those intense features.

Ever since she had first seen him, he had constantly been on her mind. He was in her every thought. It was the

thought of not only seeing him again but having to feed from him that left her body in a constant state of arousal. She had never been one with a high sex drive—having only slept with one other person in her life. She had thought it was her health problems that stopped her from enjoying life to its fullest, when, in fact, it was because of what she was. As a hybrid, she should have been surviving on the blood of another, not those damn vitamin D tablets the doctors had told her she needed.

All her life, Ebony had been lied to. Through no fault of their own, the people that had raised her hadn't known the truth, either. What she had said to Rema had been true: she didn't blame anybody for what her life had been like. How could she?

Throwing back the covers on the large fourposter bed, Ebony slipped out. Her bare feet cold on the wooden floor, she walked towards the full-length mirror that she had stood in front of with her sisters the night before. Then, she had seen a hint of who she really was. She'd seen the possibility of a life so far removed from the one she'd been brought up to believe she had wanted.

This time, with no one else in the room, Ebony truly looked at herself. Now, instead of seeing the pathetic creature she'd grudgingly gazed at in the mirror in the bathroom at the bar, she saw something completely different. Although not fully healed—which, as her sisters had informed her, would only come from feeding—she still looked ten times better than she had before. Gone were the dark circles around her eyes. Gone was the grey shade to her skin, and gone were her stormy grey eyes. Instead, the grey was now tinged with brilliant blue. Not quite the bright blue that graced the eyes of Nathan, Ivory, Rema, and scarlet, but blue nonetheless.

On some level, Ebony felt she should be missing her old life, that she should really be questioning everything she had been told. She had only heard of beings like night-walkers and **werewolves** and warlocks in movies, yet when she really thought about it, she believed every single word. It felt like coming home to know that she wasn't just worthless, unwanted, and unneeded. To know that, in fact, her new reality was the complete opposite.

Here, in front of the mirror, Ebony saw herself—her true self—and, for once, liked what she saw reflected back at her. She may have hated every single day that led to this moment but, in a way, it had been worth it.

Giving herself a brief smile, Ebony turned and headed towards the bathroom, eager for a small luxury that she hadn't had since she was small: a long, hot shower.

Maybe once she was clean and fresh she could pluck up the courage to talk to Nathan about the whole feeding thing. A subject that certainly made her nervous.

Forty-five minutes later, cleaner than she had ever been in her life, Ebony walked down the grand staircase of the mansion. Dressed in new clothes that her sisters had kindly provided, she went in search of her next meal. And by meal, she meant Nathan.

In the time she'd spent in the shower, Ebony had managed to build up enough courage to seek him out, although every nerve in her body was on edge. She felt like a teenager with a crush, only the feelings were far more intense. It was hard to describe, but she felt connected to him somehow. How, she did not know, but from the moment he had walked in to her bedroom, she had felt something click into place. Something about him called to her, and she didn't have the strength to fight it. It may have been the way he'd demanded that she feed from him, or

the fact that he was the most gorgeous guy she had ever seen.

Nathan was old school—in the sense that he was old. That's what Ivory had told her. She had said that he was almost as old as their mother would have been, if she had still been alive. He had been Captain of the Nightwalker Guard for over a hundred years and took his job very seriously. Both Scarlett and Ivory saw him as more of an uncle/brother figure, yet Ebony felt differently. A huge part of Ebony was glad. She'd never been the jealous type, yet she could tell she would be with Nathan. Daft really, when she didn't even know him. Didn't know how he felt about her. For all she knew, he could see her as simply his queen's daughter. A lost girl that required nothing more than protection.

As Ebony reached the bottom of the wooden staircase, she marvelled at the beauty of the hall. Dark mahogany wood was everywhere—the staircase, the panelling lining the walls, the doors, and even the floors. It would take her weeks, maybe months, to map her way around the stunning mansion.

Noise erupted behind a door that had been left ajar. Curiosity had her moving towards it, though she was afraid of what she might see. Peering through the gap. Ebony first saw a large snooker table. The ordinary red and yellow balls were scattered across its surface, and a large form bent over the table, cue stick in hand, aiming to strike one with the white. Ebony was just about to push her way into the room when Ivory's lyrical voice sounded.

"Oh, Bishop, seriously." Her voice sounded annoyed. Ebony thought about stepping away and leaving them to their privacy, but she stayed. For some reason, she felt the need to watch.

"Ivory, I swear you are pushing me to a place you will not like. I've given you time. Answer the damn question." The other voice surely belonged to the mysterious Bishop. Ebony had never met him, but from what she had heard, he never left Ivory's side, and didn't allow any other male near her.

"I'm not answering that." Ivory's tone had become higher in pitch, and Ebony watched her move around the table to stand in front of Bishop. The male towered over her, his build huge. He looked like he belonged on a body-building stage.

"Listen, *Princess*, I've had it with your games. Had it with being toyed with." He loomed over her, and for a second, Ebony felt a twinge of fear for her new sister.

"I'm done," he stated, and turned his back on Ivory.

"Don't you dare walk away from me!" Ivory called out after him. "Get back here this instant!" she shouted, before she stomped around the table, cutting him off.

"Move, Ivory." he growled.

"Make me," she countered, and then grinned. Ebony smiled. She knew Ivory was spunky, but to piss off a guy that size meant she had balls—big ones.

Only... the look in Bishop's eyes worried Ebony. There was a spark there, one that made Ebony wonder whether, if Ivory were to notice it, she would have backed away. His voice, deep and husky, made Ebony shiver. She suddenly felt like an interloper on their discussion.

"Oh, I will," he rumbled, before his hands shot out and grabbed Ivory by the waist, his hands so large they wrapped around it easily. With one move, he had her picked up and sat on the edge of the snooker table, his own body planted firmly between her thighs.

"What the hell, Bishop. Get the hell off me," she cried out, although she didn't struggle. Instead, she glared at him.

"You've led me on long enough, Ivory," he growled again. "Now it's my turn."

"Your turn for what?" she whispered, her eyes wide now. "Stay away, Bishop." When he did no such thing, Ivory threw her hands into the air. "That's it, I will never feed from you again," she argued, and lifted her chin.

"Yes, you will, Princess," he answered. A grin played across his lips. "You crave what only I can give you, and as much as you resent it, you can't—*won't*—go to anyone else."

Ivory bristled. Clenching her fists, she again glared at Bishop. "Yes. I. Can," she stated.

"Just try it," Bishop growled.

"I will," she fired back, and Ebony winced. This wasn't going to end as Ivory wanted.

"Then..." he breathed, and leaned in, "they are dead."

Ivory gasped. "You wouldn't!"

"Watch me," he growled again, his voice lower in tone. "No one else touches you, Ivory. Understand?"

"But...What...?" she stuttered, only to have Bishop close the gap between them, their lips millimetres apart.

"It's simple, Ivory. You. Are. Mine!"

E bony swallowed and shivered again. Any fear she had that Ivory was in danger was gone with one look at Bishop's face. He worshiped Ivory—a fact her sister knew and had played on. Only now, it was time for payback. With her arms held at her side, Ebony watched as Bishop's lips descended, taking, controlling, and possessing, until her sister whimpered and purred in response.

This was passion, and as much as Ivory had fought against it, she needed it just as much as Bishop needed her.

"Enjoying the show?" The whispered voice caressed her ear, making Ebony jump. A scream formed in her throat, but never made it out as a large, callused hand pressed against her mouth.

"Shhhhh, it's only me." Ebony knew exactly who *me* was. Every sense had come alive the moment he'd touched her. His scent overtook her senses and made her forget what she was doing stood in the hallway.

"They've been driving each other wild for months now," Nathan murmured as they watched Ivory and Bishop. Her sister was now spread across the snooker table, her hands holding Bishop's head as he kissed down her throat. Ebony turned her head. It felt wrong to be spying on her sister. Yet being here, watching something she shouldn't with a man that made her feel things felt... well, sexy.

"You don't like to watch?" he asked, and all Ebony could do was shrug. His hand had moved from her mouth and now cupped her neck, his thumb brushing up and down over her pulse.

"We nightwalkers are very sexual beings, Ebony. It's in our nature," he admitted, yet he moved away from the open door. She let him lead the way, thankful he didn't make her watch. She had never been a voyeur, although she wasn't opposed to watching porn.

"Are you ok, Ebony?" Nathan asked as they walked into a small office. One wall was filled with screens, and the other was dominated by a huge desk. Embarrassingly, Ebony's thoughts had turned to what it would be like to watch porn with Nathan.

"Err, yeah. I'm fine, thank you," she answered as nonchalantly as she could, but she couldn't stop the blush from

climbing up her cheeks. He stopped just inside the room and turned her to face him. His hand was still on her neck. She found it comforting.

He watched her for a moment, his bright eyes taking in every detail, even the blush, and Ebony shivered again.

"Are you cold?" he asked. She shook her head, suddenly unable to form any words. How do you start a conversation with a man that you not only thought was gorgeous but also wanted to feed from? And how would she even do it? She had no control over her new gnashers—hell, she had no idea how they came down. It wasn't as if she could use magic. She was no Harry Potter, that was for sure.

As if knowing what was on her mind, Nathan asked,

"Do you want to feed, little one?" His voice had lowered in tone again. Its raw masculinity hit her nerve endings, and those butterflies she had before, now took off. Their wings beating sending her equilibrium into a spin.

"Yes," she admitted, her blush now burning her skin. "Though I don't know how. My, err, fangs... Well..."

"Shhhh," he soothed. He cupped her face with his hands. His gaze sought hers and locked. "This will help." His words penetrated her mind and at the same time were forgotten as his lips descended on her own. His kiss was a slow, sensual glide of lip on lip. His tongue flicked out and caressed the seam of her lips, asking for entrance. Ebony gave it to him. His taste was like nothing she had experienced before, and she whimpered with need. Wanting more. Needing more...

His hands had moved from her face and now held her waist in a vice-like grip, pulling her body flush against his own. Ebony's own hands now rested upon a very large and very hard chest. As the kiss continued, she fought the need to rub herself against his hard body like a purring kitten. A

groan of displeasure flew from her throat as Nathan pulled away and ended the kiss.

"See," he said, and grinned. At first, Ebony frowned, but then she felt the sharp pressure of something against her lower lip. Removing her hand from Nathan's chest, she swiped a finger across her mouth, gasping when she felt the tip of her fangs.

"As I said, little one, we are very sexual creatures. Our true selves appear when we are, for lack of a better term, turned on." Nathan's fingers stroked her cheek, and then moved a piece of hair from her face.

"Shall we get you fed?" he asked, and Ebony could do little but nod. Her new fangs felt strange and bulky. Taking her hand, Nathan led her to his large chair. He sat and pulled her straight onto his lap. She gasped as she felt the all too obvious sign of his own arousal hard and proud against her arse. Pulling her tight against him, he placed his large forearm in front of her.

Ebony just looked at it, unsure of what to do or say. She didn't want to hurt him, and even now, the idea of drinking someone's blood felt wrong.

"Ebony?" he murmured, and she looked up into his bright eyes. "You won't hurt me. You need to feed. I know it sounds strange and wrong, but once you do it, you will see," he urged, and once again pushed his arm into her hands.

"Just take hold of my arm, and then chomp down," he said with a grin. "It's easy."

When he put it like that... Yes, it sounded easy, only Ebony still couldn't imagine herself doing it. As she sat there, her gaze flicking between his arm and his beautiful face, she realised that she could put it off forever, but the outcome would still be the same. She would still need to feed, and from the determined look on the Nathan's face, it

would still be him that provided her much-needed meal. With an encouraging nod from Nathan, Ebony looked back at his large forearm. Using both hands, she held it gently, her thumbs stroking the surprisingly soft skin. His veins were prominent and made it clear that he led a life that was more than active.

Taking one long, deep breath, Ebony bent her head and brought his arm up to meet her lips. At first, she licked his skin, surprised by the pleasant saltiness, and before she had time to back out, she opened her mouth, and guided her new fangs to slide through soft flesh. Instantly, her mouth was filled with Nathan's warm blood.

Instead of being repulsed like she thought she would be, she found herself surprised by the flavour. The moment it hit her tongue and flowed to the back of her throat, she was addicted. It was thick, warm, and pleasure-inducing. As it settled in her stomach, her body reacted, burning her from the inside out. Ebony couldn't stop the moan that left her throat as she gripped his forearm more firmly and took a harder pull on his vein.

Ebony felt Nathan's free arm wrap around her, pulling her closer to him. She felt his lips against her hair, heard the unmistakable male groan of pure need that whispered from his lips.

"That's it, little one, take what you need," he growled.

Ebony closed her eyes as she continued to feed, her body becoming heavy and lethargic. Her lips swept over the puncture mark she had created on his arm as she finally pulled away. She rested her head in his palm, unable to lift it. The burning she had felt continued to spread throughout her body, until even the tips of her fingers and toes tingled. Yet she felt like she could sleep for a week.

"What's wrong with me?"

Ebony's words were slurred as exhaustion took hold. She forced her eyes to open and looked up into Nathan's bright blue ones. Even her vision seemed blurry. Panic started to set in as she tried to move but was unable to do so.

"Why can't I move? What have you done to me?" Her voice was a mere whisper, but when she focused on Nathan's face, he didn't seem panicked. In fact, he smiled and stroked the hair away from her face.

"Shhh, it's okay, little one. It's just your body adjusting to its new diet." The deep, husky sound of his voice, along with the stroking of her hair, had Ebony closing her eyes, wanting to give in the darkness creeping in.

"Rest now, little one, I've got you." With little strength left to fight, Ebony let the darkness take her, knowing she was safe in Nathan's arms. Right where she wanted to be.

11

JUSTIN HAD BEEN WATCHING the mansion for the past five hours. Surprisingly, nothing much at happened. His master —his king—had always insinuated that the nightwalkers flaunted themselves in front of both mortals and the immortal races. Though, from what he had observed tonight, it seemed to be the complete opposite. The only comings and goings that happened were the postman, and many deliverymen, which seemed excessive. But from what he heard of the princesses, they were prone to the mortal habit of shopping.

With everything he'd been told, and believed, about the princesses, it was only now that Justin began to doubt whether all of it had been true. His king had created a prophesy among the warlocks that the three females would be the downfall of his race.

Gregori seemed adamant that they had to be destroyed, and that alone gave Justin pause. His king had not attacked any other immortal race outwardly. He enjoyed more subtle ways of gaining power. He had allies—they were few, but

powerful, and would follow the king into whatever battle awaited.

Gregori had secrets, of that Justin was well aware. But what the king didn't realise, was that Justin was privy to some of those secrets. Like how this sudden interest in destroying the princesses had raised suspicions on how he had gained power in the past. Justin was also aware that the females weren't just an enemy, they were also the only heirs to the nightwalker throne. But that wasn't all he had found out.

His king was also the father of the three prophesized females, which made them not only a hybrid of both warlock and nightwalker, but also more powerful than any immortal could comprehend.

Justin's conscience had come into play a lot of late. The things he had been asked to do by his king, he had performed with no questions asked. Although now, with each day that passed, he felt as if he was losing more and more of his soul. It had started as a black smudge that then grew and grew, and if it continued on this path, there would be no way back. But what choice did he have? Gregori gave no second chances and was not a believer in mercy. He had witnessed that in the **were** that had been fused to the ballroom wall, making him a new part of the decoration.

There was a fate Justin didn't want for himself, but it would take more that and is back on his own kind to escape but Gregori had planned so for now you would do as it is master bidded and pray that once done he could be redeemed but he didn't hold out much hope.

As he watched the house, the street lights came on. The

sun had set not long ago, and Justin now hoped he would see some sort of movement from within the mansion. It didn't take long until he was rewarded. Shopping bags in hand, a small woman walked out the front door and headed down the street. He could tell she wasn't one of the princesses, but she was all he had in that moment. Getting out of his battered, nondescript Ford Mondeo, Justin collected his mobile phone from his pocket. Pressing speed dial, he placed it to his ear and waited.

"I have a way in," Justin stated. "I will need a collection from my current location."

He waited as he heard the response on the phone and nodded before he answered,

"Yes, she's alone. I will relay the message." He paused. "My lord, it will be done."

With that, the connection was cut Justin palmed the mobile before he placed it back inside his pocket, tightened his jacket around him, and walked in the direction of his new prey. He felt uneasy about what he was about to do, but he had little choice. Gregori wanted a way to get to the girls, and Justin had found it. He just hoped he didn't lose his soul in the process.

NATHAN WATCHED Ebony as she slept in his arms. As soon as she'd finished feeding, she had passed out. Now, he had the chance to study her, watch her, and learn every feature, every freckle.

The feeding experience had been one of the most intense situations he had ever been in—hell, even the kiss had riled him up. Ebony displayed a passion she wasn't even aware of, and that called out to him. Nathan had never thought of himself as the mating kind, not when his life had always been devoted to the Royals, but now... now every nightwalker instinct in his mind, gut, and even soul, drew him to her. It was like, from the moment he had truly seen her outside that bar, they had been connected, and with every look, every touch, that connection had reduced in length, pushing them closer together and sealing a bond that shouldn't happen.

He was a guard, she was a princess—not a good match, especially in the eyes of the council. Yet Nathan couldn't find it in himself to care. In his long existence, he had never felt more complete and at peace as he did now, with Ebony

healing and fed from his blood and now resting in his arms. She fit him as no one else ever had. Being as old as he was, he had sought out many women for pleasure in his time. They had temporarily sated the itch, but as with all his kind, the lack of a mate had left a hole in his soul.

Warm breath whispered across his neck as Ebony let out a small snore, and he couldn't help but chuckle. It was the little things in life, things that Ebony was reminding him of, that he now realised he missed. There was simply no other explanation for how quickly Nathan was becoming attached to her, how much he thought about her since he had returned her home.

His issue now was the council. They had already made plans for the girls to be married off, so they keep control of ruling over the nightwalker race. The thought of Ebony being matched with another male made Nathan's chest hurt, and anger boiled in his gut.

They barely knew each other. She was younger than him by a long shot, and she was a Royal, but that didn't stop the possessive thoughts that now ran rampant through his mind.

She was his. It was a fact cemented in stone, and one he wouldn't be afraid of enforcing.

Nathan was pulled from his thoughts by the alarm going off on his desk. Moving slightly, making sure he didn't disturb Ebony, he picked up the headpiece that connected to all of the Elite. Placing it around his ear, he responded.

"Elite One, what's the status?" he asked.

"Nathan..." an out of breath voice called over the system, "been... taken." The static corrupted the signal, so only a few words could be heard.

"Curtis, please repeat," Nathan answered, only to have

Bishop rush through the door. Luckily, Ebony stayed asleep, the feeding having knocked her out cold.

"Nathan," Bishop said, his fangs fully descended. He wasn't sure if it was from his earlier session with Ivory, or whatever had Curtis in a panic.

"What the fuck is going on?" he demanded.

"It's Rema," Bishop rushed out. "She's been taken."

"What!" Nathan roared, and this time, Ebony woke with a scream. Nathan held her tight in his arms, rocking her until she settled again, before he stood and placed her in his seat. Immediately, he felt the loss of her, but now his gut churned for his sister.

"Come," he ordered, leaving the office and moving across the hall to the snooker room, which was now devoid of Ivory, although the scent of arousal still remained.

"Tell me." Nathan folded his large arms across his chest and looked at his second-in-command.

"Rema left to go to the shops, like she always does, only she was followed. She called Curtis from the shop to tell him she didn't feel safe, but then didn't respond to any more calls. Curtis went after her, but only found her handbag. The other elites are searching the streets for any sign of her now."

Nathan started to pace, worry, anger, and frustration boiling inside him. "How the fuck has this happened? Do we know who took her?" Nathan growled out, only to hear Curtis's voice, slightly distorted from static, over the headset.

"Nathan."

"Curtis, do you have her?" he snapped. Worry for his sister was eating at him. She had always been protected by the Guard, and he had no idea why anyone would want her. His heart almost stopped at a thought that flitted in through

his mind. Unless the same people that wanted the princess had something to do with it.

"No. I'm sorry, there is no sign of Rema, but we have someone that will lead us to her."

"Who?" Nathan asked through clenched teeth.

"A warlock," Curtis answered. Nathan's hunch may have been right, and this warlock would pay the ultimate price if anything happened to his sister.

13

EBONY WAS FLOATING in a world of peace and pleasure. Her body felt light, with no aches or pains. Any dizziness she had felt before was gone. Instead, deep within her, she felt a throb. Of what, she had no idea, but it was there, eager for her to call out to it. She knew that she only had to ask, and it would do her bidding.

In her mind's eye, it looked like a small speck of light, that with almost no encouragement, could spread and encompass everything. Ebony wasn't afraid, though. In fact, she felt the opposite. The throb inside her felt like protection and power all-in-one, and all it would take was Ebony to embrace it.

And she would have if she wasn't then abruptly shaken awake.

"Ebony, wake up," Ivory's voice called out, and she felt herself being shaken until her head connected with the arm of the chair she had been placed in.

"Ow! Bloody hell," she reacted, holding her head and sitting up in the big, luxurious chair. Its leather was soft yet still squeaked when she moved. At first, she couldn't

remember where she was or how she had got there, until a certain male's bright blue eyes and kissable lips entered her mind.

"Oh!" Ebony blurted, and then blushed.

"Yeah, I'm not going to ask how or why you are in Nathan's office, or why you are blushing like I just caught you doing something naughty." Ivory grinned. "Up you get, Sleeping Beauty, there's been a situation."

Ebony rubbed her eyes and slowly stood. Sleep still drifted at the edge of her consciousness, and if she wanted, she could easily get back into the chair and pass out again. Only, the look of worry on Ivory's face made her pause.

"What's wrong?"

"Rema," Ivory admitted, and turned. "She was kidnapped whilst she was out at the shops."

"What! Oh, my god. Who would do that?" Ebony asked, and followed Ivory into the hall. Her sister didn't head to the stairs or the snooker room, but instead moved towards another wooden door. One that looked just like the rest.

"We have an idea, and the boys have managed to grab someone to torture into submission," Ivory replied, and pushed through the door. On the other side lay an extensive library that would be any book-nerd's wet dream.

"Wow," Ebony blurted out, gaining a chuckle from Scarlett who sat on a sofa in front of a large fire place.

"Yeah, it has that effect—just the way we like it." She smiled. "Come sit, we have much to talk about."

Ebony nodded, but instead of heading to the sofa where both her sisters now sat, she went to an overstuffed chair and climbed in, sinking into the cushions and feeling immediately at home.

"Told ya," Scarlett chimed, only to have Ivory scowl. "Shut up."

"What?" Ebony asked.

"Scarlett chose that chair for you, said you would be drawn to it." Ivory pouted. "No fair, you can see the sodding future."

"Only snippets, and stop scowling," Scarlett grinned, "it gives you crow's feet." That comment earned a gasp from Ivory, before she dived off the sofa to study her face in the closest mirror.

"Cow," Ivory spat as she returned.

"Tart," Scarlett quipped.

"Err, ladies, sorry to interrupt, but what do you need to talk to me about?" Ebony asked, somehow knowing they would have bickered for hours if left to it. Not that she minded—listening to them felt good, especially when they included her.

"Sorry," Scarlett answered, and patted the seat next to her for Ivory to sit again.

"Okay, I'm going to give you the short version, seeing as we may not have much time."

"Okay..." Ebony felt nervous, on edge, but after everything she had been told so far, she was now a believer.

"Right, our mum, the Queen, shacked up with a warlock. She thought it was love. He didn't."

"He was an arse," Ivory added.

Scarlett nodded. "Yes, he was. When Mum found out she was pregnant, she went to the council, and they advised her—"

"Advised... Ha! They ordered her to abort us."

"Yeah, that too. Will you shut up now?" Scarlett barked at Ivory.

"Fine," Ivory huffed. She folded her arms and sat back on the sofa, her bottom lip protruding so far that Ebony could have played a tune on it.

"Mum, in response, made plans to have us without the council or the warlock knowing. Turns out, Daddy is the big show, and the only reason he got with Mum was for her power."

"Power?" Ebony questioned.

"Yes. Every nightwalker, since the birth of our race, is born with some sort of power. Ivory is good at mind manipulation. I can see certain things in the future."

"What about me?" Ebony asked as she moved to the edge of her chair, eager to hear more.

"We don't know. Well, not yet." Scarlett admitted, and smiled slightly.

"How do you know all of this? That Mum died having us."

"She left us a book that explained many things, and what wasn't in the book, both Rema and Nathan taught us," Scarlett answered, and pulled a battered leather book from under one of the sofa's pillows, a triquetra symbol embossed into the cover.

"A book? And that tells you what, exactly?"

"Well, for starters its helped us understand our nightwalker power, but it's also taught us that, as hybrids, we have access to a lot more. Ebony, our father is the leader of the warlocks. His blood is as pure as our mother's was."

"Which means what?" Ebony asked again, not really understanding where the conversation was going.

"It means we have more power than even him. We are a product of two different energies that combined."

"And now we are united as three, we are able to access it," Ivory blurted again but she too was on the edge of the chair. Ebony wasn't sure what to make of the information. How do you believe in something like magic when you've only just been made aware of immortal beings?

"What does this have to do with Rema being taken?"

"Simple. Our daddy wants us. He thinks by kidnapping her, we will agree to his terms," Scarlett answered, ending with a growl. "We will, of course. Rema is the closest thing we have to a mother, there is no way we are leaving her there."

"Agreed," Ebony replied.

Scarlett continued, "However, we do have an advantage. Dear, old Daddy thinks we don't know anything about our power. In fact, so does the Elite Guard. They seem to believe we are oblivious to everything that has been going on. We know all about the council and their plans of *marriage*." She spat out that last word with venom.

"Who are the council?" Ebony asked, her mind a whirr from everything that had been said so far.

"Err, that's a conversation for another time. Nathan and the guys are now planning on getting Rema back using the prisoner they have just acquired. They caught themselves a warlock. But because we are princesses, and female, they won't include us in their plans."

Scarlett looked excited, and Ebony didn't know if that worried her or not. Her sisters were, pretty much, still strangers to her, but they were the only family she had. In the time she had been at the mansion, she had been told she was a princess that drank blood, and now had powers, almost like she should be in her very own version of Harry-bloody-Potter. She had also drunk someone's blood. And enjoyed it. And really wanted to do it again, along with other rather naughty things, to the male that had provided the meal.

"So, what are you planning?" Ebony asked, unsure if she wanted to hear the answer.

"Simple." Scarlett grinned. "You distract and gain infor-

mation from Nathan. Ivory will deal with Bishop, like she usually does, and I will go talk to our new guest," Scarlett stated, before adding, "Take this, Ebony. You need to get up to speed as well, because when we meet our father, we are going to need all the power we have." Scarlett handed over the book. Its heavy weight fell into Ebony's hands, and she pulled it close.

"Why does he want us?" Ebony asked, the leather book against her chest. Her fingers stroked the cover, tracing the pattern on its surface. The leather felt warm to the touch, and the smell gave her the briefest glimpse of a memory that she couldn't hold on to. The leather on the cover matched the leather of her bracelet, and for Ebony, that confirmed she was right where she was meant to be.

"We are his heirs, yes?" Both Ivory and Ebony nodded in response to Scarlett's question, and she continued,

"As such, we hold power in our bloodline, but if something should happen to us, our power would go to our next blood relative."

"Our father," Ebony whispered, connecting the dots. "That's why he wanted me dead in the alley, that's why he wants us all dead. He just wants the power we hold."

"Exactly," Scarlett agreed. "That, and there may be a tiny prophecy about us, too. One that is giving dear, old dad a case of the twitchy arse syndrome." Scarlett added, "And frankly, he's annoying me, so I would rather deal with the old Croat sooner rather than later."

"I'm in," Ivory stated. "I like my life. I'm not overly keen on dying."

"Ebony?" both sisters asked, seeing the worry on her face as she looked at the leather book. Determination had started to set in. This was her family now, a family she had prayed for since she was little.

"I've only just found you guys—well, you found me. And for the first time in my life, I finally have somewhere that feels like home. He's barking if he thinks I've survived this long only for him to take it away from me. I'm most definitely in."

Ebony felt energised by not only the conversation and learning about herself, but by her recent meal as well. Life was starting to click into place, although it was a little crazier than she ever thought it could be. But both Scarlett and Ivory were right. This man that claimed to be there father wanted them dead. So, they had a choice: either bend over and take it or make him do the bending.

Settling further into the chair, Ebony opened the book she had been given. Her sisters headed out to do what they needed. Ebony was to wait for Nathan to come find her, and, as instructed, use her feminine wiles—like Ivory did—to get information. Only Ebony wasn't going to be faking her interest in Nathan. If her life was on the line, she needed to enjoy every second she had.

If that meant taking advantage of the Captain of the Elite Guard, stripping him butt naked and having her way with him, then she would most definitely take one for the team. She might even be persuaded to take two. After all, it was Nathan himself that had said nightwalkers were sexually charged creatures. She would find out exactly how sexual he was and put it to the test.

Time for Ebony to become the princess she was born to be.

NATHAN GROWLED in frustration as the warlock took blow after blow from Bishop yet never caved. They had been attempting to interrogate him for two hours now, yet he healed and withstood everything. Bar having his head ripped off by Bishop.

"Bishop, stop. This is getting us nowhere," Nathan called out to his friend. Brute force obviously wasn't the way to go, although he felt like beating the little shit himself. Instead, he pulled out a chair and sat down in front of the warlock.

"So, are you going to tell us where you have taken the female, or are we just going to kill you?" Nathan asked calmly, watching the warlock carefully. They had strapped both hands behind his back and taped his fingers to his palms. Warlocks had always been tricky, and he wouldn't risk any of his team with one the mansion—never mind the princesses upstairs.

"I have nothing to say to you," the warlock spat out. "Though I will speak to one of the three."

"Like fuck you will," Bishop growled out. Nathan held out a palm to stop his friend advancing and doing what they

had threatened. There was nothing messier than decapitation.

"You have zero hope of speaking to them," Nathan admitted. He would rather face the hot fires of hell than let Ebony anywhere near this male. He wouldn't allow any of them near him, but any thought of Ebony in danger shot his blood pressure up to a dangerous level and made him want to break things. Ideally things that belonged on the bodies of warlocks or **weres**.

"I have a message for them from Gregori, Lord of the warlocks," the male said calmly. His eyes, brown with hints of gold, flashed. He may have been able to heal himself of some of his injuries, but the bruising and split lip remained. Blood dripped down his chin and made Nathan think of Ebony and their feeding earlier. His body reacted instantly at the memory of her fangs in his skin and the pull on his vein. Nathan stood and walked behind the warlock, not wanting him to see any reaction from him—or to have to explain himself.

"Well, you can give the message to us and we will pass it along," he growled out. "Where is the female you took?" Nathan asked again, his fists clenching, wanting nothing more than to wrap his hands around the warlock's neck and squeeze.

"She will be with my lord," the warlock stated, and then closed his eyes—his only way of ending the conversation. With a nod, Bishop headed for the door of the small, cell-like room they had created for situations like this, Nathan following close behind. Once they had both stepped out of the room, Bishop turned and threw a fist to the wall, the punch breaking through the brickwork easily, as if it were plasterboard.

"He will not get anywhere near Ivory, Nathan. I won't

allow it." Bishop's growled voice, laced with barely-contained fury, gave Nathan pause. He had never seen him almost lose control on his other side yet now he seemed on edge.

"Bishop, calm down. He won't get to her; he won't get to any of the girls. What is wrong with you?" Nathan asked as they walked towards the stairs that would take them up to his office. He needed to speak to the rest of the Elite Guard and find Ebony. He needed to see her again, needed *her* with an intensity that worried him.

"I don't know. I've been on edge since I saw Ivory earlier. I swear she's bewitched me somehow," Bishop admitted, and rubbed his fist, the broken, bloody skin quickly healing.

"Get it under control, my friend. This is not the time for you to lose your shit. I need you focused," Nathan ordered, but patted his friend on the back. "Get the rest of the team together. The warlock will cave," Nathan said with confidence. "We will get Rema back," he stated finally, before moving through his office, stopping only briefly to check the camera feeds. As hoped, he quickly found Ebony's location.

He couldn't fight the need he had to see her anymore. Regardless of his worry for Rema, there was little he could do until they located where she had been taken. It ate at him that he couldn't do more, but with the Elite Guard bombarding the captured warlock, it wouldn't be long before he cracked.

Pushing his way through the door of his office, Nathan walked through the hallway and headed straight for the library. He remembered the day they had insisted they have it, and for weeks they had received books by the truck-loads. They had always been readers, and the library had become their haven. Now Ebony was here. He was glad to see she had been shown the library and was settling in well.

Not bothering to knock, Nathan strolled in. Instead of a gasp of surprise, as he had expected and hoped for, he watched as she calmly placed down the book she was reading and looked up at him with a smile. A smile which both calmed him and raised his blood pressure. His body reacted instantly to her presence and made him desperate to take her in his arms.

"Ebony," he breathed, and stalked closer, until she was almost within touching distance. He had to force himself to stop. She was still new to his world, to being a nightwalker, and would not understand why, after such a short time, he believed—no, he knew—she was his. From her response to his kiss in the office earlier, he had hope that she felt something towards him. But it was something he would have to take slowly. The last thing he wanted, or needed, was to scare her off.

"You are well?" he asked. "Was everything ok after you fed?" He had hated to leave her, but he'd had no choice. There was nothing he wanted more than to have had her wake in his arms, and maybe continue with the kiss they had started.

"Yes, I am well, thank you," she answered, and smiled wider. "I feel normal."

"Normal?" Nathan questioned. That wasn't a word he would usually place with a female that had fed. Although, she wasn't a typical nightwalker; she was a hybrid. He watched as she uncurled her legs from under her and got up from the comfy chair. She was dressed in the same jeans and t-shirt from earlier. Her hair was loose and cascaded down her back in dark waves that he longed to run his fingers through. He felt his fingers twitch in response. As she stepped closer, he had to hold back from pulling her

into him. To, instead, let her step as close as she felt comfortable.

"Yes, normal, and for me, that's the best I've felt since I was little." Slowly, Ebony tucked a stray strand of hair behind her ear, and continued her explanation.

"For as long as I can remember, I have always had health issues. I was pushed from one foster family to next because they couldn't deal with them, or simply didn't want to. I've lived by taking vitamin D tablets to combat my photophobia, and have survived on little food."

She sighed and stepped closer. "No one would have known that I needed the blood of another to make me function healthily. So, yeah, I'm finally feeling normal—like I should have been feeling all along."

Surprising Nathan again, Ebony placed her hands against his chest, pushed herself up onto her toes, and pressed her lips to his own in the briefest of kisses. Nathan's eyes closed at the sensation but snapped open as soon as the connection was lost.

"I have you to thank for saving my life... Not once, but twice." She was still so close he could feel her body heat. Not letting himself think about the consequences, Nathan placed his hands around Ebony's waist and tugged her even closer, enjoying the feel of her curves now pressed against him. Since her feeding, she had gone from being thin and malnourished to now sporting curves that made Nathan's mouth water. She fit him with perfection, like she had been created simply for him. He felt her hands rest gently against his chest as she tilted her head to look up at him. Lifting a hand, he cupped her cheek, stroking his thumb across the soft skin.

"Your eyes," he murmured, transfixed by the change.

"What about them?" she whispered back, turning her head slightly into his palm.

"They are no longer grey," Nathan answered. Her new eye colour still wasn't the simple bright blue that identified a nightwalker. Instead, they were a shimmering blue with silver specks that sparkled.

"Stunning," he murmured as he bent his head and touched his lips to hers once again. Her taste was addictive, and he had craved it constantly since their last kiss. He doubted that he would ever tire of it. In fact, it was the opposite. His need for it would only increase with time, along with the intensity.

Nathan smiled into the kiss as Ebony responded, her small hands gripping the fabric of his shirt until they made fists. Whimpers of pleasure escaped her throat, and he felt her knees weaken slightly, causing him to hold her tighter to him as he deepened the kiss. As soon as his tongue slid across the seam of her lips, she opened them immediately, granting him access and the ability to take control.

Although control was a fickle thing—he was at the edge of his own. Balancing like on a tight rope, needing only a slight push to send him into oblivion. Only the oblivion Ebony would grant him would no doubt send him to heights he had never been to before. He wanted to fall, wanted to let go and be just a male worshipping his mate.

Nathan reluctantly ended the kiss, breaking the connection. Ebony moaned, her breathing now heavy and her body now totally relying on Nathan's to keep her upright. Sometime during his kiss, she had closed her eyes, and now, as she opened them, he saw a flash of disappointment. She wanted to know why he had stopped—a question he now asked himself as he saw her flushed cheeks, swollen lips, and eyes filled with heat. He would not take advantage of

Ebony, no matter how much he longed to lose himself in her softness.

"Nathan?" she questioned, her voice quiet. "Is everything ok?"

What did he say to that? Should he admit that he wouldn't take advantage of her, or should he say they can't, even though she could feel his own reaction to her touch and kiss? It all stemmed down to who they were. She was a Royal and he was a guard. That there was a match that shouldn't happen—couldn't happen—especially if the council found out.

"We can't, Ebony," was all that left his mouth. "We shouldn't go any further."

He watched as her beautiful features frowned and she pulled away and out of his arms.

"You don't want me? You will kiss me, even feed me and make demands of me, yet you don't want me? What kind of game are you playing, Nathan?" Her voice rose higher in pitch with each word, and he struggled to find the words that would calm her. All he wanted was to pull her back into his arms and finish what they started. His conflict was driving him insane. One moment he was ready to take that step, and the next, he wouldn't.

"I want you, Ebony, that's never been in doubt."

"So what's the issue?" she snapped, her arms now folded across her chest.

"You're a Royal. I'm... not," he admitted, and could no longer hold her gaze. Instead, he looked at the paintings on the wall behind her. Only the feel of her hands on his chest brought it back to her beautiful face.

"I don't care," she said simply, and he frowned. He held back his reply and let her talk. Fighting his instincts, he let her lead the way.

"Yes, I'm a Royal, but I only found that out yesterday. It doesn't change who I am. And yes, you are a guard, but you aren't just any guard, you're the captain, and that doesn't change who *you* are: a loyal male who puts his own life on the line for those under his protection." She smiled and placed her small hand into his large one. Slowly, and still smiling up at him, she brought it to her lips, kissing the knuckles.

"What we are does not define who we are, Nathan. The truth is, I'm just a girl, looking up at a guy, hoping he likes her just as much as she likes him." Her words took far too long to penetrate his skull.

"You like me?" he whispered, and once the words were out of his mouth, he winced. He sounded stupid.

"I wouldn't have kissed you back if I didn't, Nathan," she replied, a smile twitching her lips. She interlocked her fingers with his own, the ones she had just kissed, before she moved, tugging him after her. In that moment, Nathan realised that he would follow Ebony anywhere. He had found his mate, and she wanted him back.

"Where are we going?" he asked as she led them out of the library and into the hall, her movements slow.

"My room, Nathan," she said confidently, and that was all it took for Nathan's control and conscience to break. In one step, he lifted her into his arms, her own wrapping around his neck, bringing her face close to his. He smiled as she squealed in surprise, but silenced it with a quick, brutal kiss, before he started up the stairs, taking them two at a time.

Possessiveness took over, and one word kept repeating in his head, over and over.

Mine.

15

Ebony held on, her arms wrapped tightly around Nathan's neck as he bolted up the stairs, taking them two at a time. She had to bite her lip to stop the giggle that threatened to escape. When he had pulled away from her and basically said no, she had been both gutted and mortified. She had acted like a tart, throwing herself at him, and he hadn't wanted her. Well, that was what she'd thought, until he had come up with his lame excuse.

Ebony honestly couldn't care less if he was a guard. She wouldn't have cared if he was a bloody bin man. Nathan, so far, had been the only man that not only showed her any attention, but cared. He had rescued her, he'd fed her, and now he kissed her like he was starving man. Ebony had already made the choice to have her way with him, so when he had backed away like he was going to leave, she had acted. And now, to her immense pleasure, he was whisking her upstairs at a speed that was making her dizzy.

In mere moments, he was stood in the centre of her new bedroom. The door had slammed shut, giving them the privacy they needed. Her mission had been to get whatever

information she could out of him, but she doubted she would be able to pull that off. Her mind instantly turned to mush when Nathan kissed her, and if things went further, she was sure she would lose all basic function.

This was the kind of male women dreamed about, and Ebony was about to put that dream to the test. Was it possible to have the kind of passion spoken about in romance novels? Hell, if the whole notion of a vampyre was real, then maybe the passion was, too. His arms tightened slightly before he removed one, letting her legs drop as he slowly lowered her to the ground. Nathan still didn't let go once her feet had hit the floor. Instead, he pulled her flush against his hard body. Moments went by as he stood staring at her, his eyes, that now familiar bright blue, blazed with heat, making Ebony's heart race.

Ebony's eyes closed as he bent forward, but instead of taking her lips like before, he laid small kisses across her cheek, moving towards her jaw, until he reached her ear. His breath whispered across the shell, an answering shiver dancing down her spine as he murmured,

"Ebony... if we start now, there is no stopping." His words caused goosebumps to rise across her whole body, and her pussy tightened.

"And once we start, there is no going back," he growled, the sound weakening her knees. "You are mine. Understand, Princess?" His voice had lowered, like it had when he had offered his vein, only now it wasn't his blood she was craving. Her panties were damp, and her nipples rubbed against the material of her bra. She wanted to answer, but the connection between her mind and mouth had severed, leaving her only able to pant and moan. His teeth nibbled the soft skin behind her ear, and Ebony's knees collapsed, but Nathan was there, collecting her once again in his arms

and carrying her over to the four-poster bed. His eyes gazed into her own as he gently laid her across the duvet, lying down next to her. Ebony's head rested on his bicep as he leaned over, pressing small kissed to her jaw once again.

"Are you going to answer me, Ebony?" she heard him ask, and she fought against the pleasure-induced haze that had taken over her mind.

"huh?" was all she was able to say, gaining a chuckle of male satisfaction that filled the room and caused butterflies to erupt in her stomach.

"Do you want this?" he asked simply, pinning her with his eyes as one hand stroked up her thigh, the heat of it branding her skin through her jeans.

"Yes," she whispered. That was all she could manage, and all that was needed, as Nathan melded his lips with hers, heating her from within. His hands were everywhere, kneading her flesh, before he made quick work of her clothing, stripping Ebony until she was left in just her bra and panties. The matching purple set had been provided to her by her sisters, and she praised their taste. That was her only thought before Nathan was back, taking control of her lips has his hands learned her body, skin to skin.

Ebony's eyes widened when he stripped himself of his own jeans and t-shirt. She almost swallowed her tongue when she realised he went commando. His body was, to her, pure perfection. Muscle stacked on muscle, with a light dusting of hair across his chest. Ebony itched to touch him, but instead just stared, open-mouthed, when she had seen his arousal. Nathan was in proportion, if not larger. Ebony's pussy clenched with need, and her mouth became dry. Yes, she'd had sex before, but her previous partner was nowhere near as large.

His touch sent sparks of pleasure shooting throughout

her body, and when his hand ventured lower, Ebony once again lost the ability to think. All she could do was feel.

Ebony's back arched as Nathan's hand moved lower, his talented fingers locating every sensitive place she had—even ones she never knew existed.

"Oh, god," she moaned when he found her soaking pussy, one large digit stroking the wet entrance before pushing in.

His chuckle in her ear made her clench as his heated words penetrated her mind,

"No, not a god, Princess. Nightwalker." He moved his finger, never letting her rest as another joined it, stretching her and building her pleasure.

"Does this feel good?" he growled. "Do you want it harder... deeper...?" Each word was echoed by the thrust of his hand. Ebony's pussy clenched with each push of his fingers, and the already unrelenting ache turned into a full-on, near-violent need.

"Just imagine, Princess..." His words, this time, whispered across her lips, his own skating across their surface, not quite making contact, and Ebony moved, seeking his mouth. He removed his fingers, and she moaned at the loss, but it soon turned into a purr of pleasure as his hips slid against hers. His huge cock pressed against her belly, and Ebony wrapped her legs around Nathan's waist in a silent bid for relief.

"Imagine my cock pressing into you." Ebony groaned, and her hips bucked. Nathan lifted slightly, letting his heavy length drop into position, the thick, engorged head pressing against her opening. She felt his hand move, taking his cock and stroking the tip up and down her swollen lips. Her sensitive clit throbbed in response, and she cried out.

"You want this," he growled, and pressed just the tip

inside her, before he pulled out. His hand still fisted his cock, pumping up and down. Her pussy had been wet before, but now she felt drenched.

"Ebony." He said her name and she finally opened her eyes to gaze into his.

"Do you want this deep inside you?" he asked. Heat, passion, and something Ebony had never seen before flashed across his face.

"Tell me, Princess, or you won't get it." To emphasise his words, he again pressed the tip inside, before removing it completely.

"Yes... God yes, Nathan. Please," she begged, and pressed her heels into his lower back, urging him to end her torment.

"That's my girl," he answered, slamming his lips against hers at the same time he thrust home, burying himself to the hilt. Ebony's body accepted him with ease. She screamed out her pleasure, and Nathan swallowed it. Her nails dug into Nathan's biceps as he set a fast pace, thrust after thrust, each more powerful than the last. Each one hitting her clit and shooting pleasure through every part of her body.

She wouldn't last, yet she didn't care. Nathan was relentless, his powerful body taking control of her own. Ebony felt something snap into place deep inside her, yet she couldn't focus on it. She felt her fangs descend, and she tasted blood —Nathan's. They'd nicked his lip.

"That's it." Nathan's thrusts became harder, more erratic. "Feed from me, baby," he panted as he exposed his neck to her. Ebony acted on instinct and struck, her fangs sinking deep. She groaned against his neck as his rich blood hit her tongue. Her body, unable to take anymore, erupted, her

orgasm shooting through her and forcing her mouth away from Nathan's neck as she screamed.

Nathan continued to thrust, prolonging her pleasure and sending sparks up her spine until he stiffened, the muscles in his neck bulging as he threw his head back and roared his own release.

Their bodies entwined, Ebony tried to breathe. Her lungs fought for air as she smiled up at Nathan's face. His answering smile hit Ebony in the chest, warming it.

"Wow," she breathed.

"You haven't seen nothing yet," Nathan answered, wrapping his arms around Ebony and rolling them over.

"We haven't finished yet, Princess, not by a long shot."

GREGORI LOOKED DOWN at the small woman in front of him and sneered. He remembered her—briefly. She had been the Lady-in-waiting to Queen Angelica, and one of the few that had helped the queen escape.

"This was not the female I wanted," he snapped, making the other warlocks in the room jump. He enjoyed the fact they were constantly on edge, unsure what he would do next. That way, they would do his bidding out of fear. He had cemented that fear when he had fused the **were** to the wall. Gregori flicked his eyes up to the still-alive mongrel, pleased to see the immortal was still kicking—literally.

"Where is Justin?" Gregori demanded, wanting to know where the male who had promised to deliver the princesses was.

"He was taken, my lord. The nightwalkers captured him," Clifford answered, his voice shaky as he bent on one knee. Clifford, although power-hungry, had been loyal so far. He was also bloodthirsty, confirmed by the bruises across the female's neck and her cut lip. He wasn't scared of getting his hands dirty, and Gregori liked that.

"He did, did he?" Annoyance laced his tone, he was still no closer to dealing with the whores that were his offspring and he had now lost a loyal servant. Standing from his throne, Gregori glided down the stairs, halting before the female. Her face tilted up, her eyes blazing with defiance.

Bending, Gregori stroked her cheek with a long nail, turning it slightly so the sharpened tip cut through the flesh. Her whimper was music to his ears. Her pain his pleasure.

"Don't worry, pet, I will take good care of you." He laughed as she screamed in pain. He bent his head down and looked her in the eye. "Scream again for me... louder this time."

SCARLETT PUSHED OPEN the wooden door to Nathan's office, pleased to see the room empty of the Captain and none of the other Elite Guards present. She knew Bishop was being dealt with by Ivory, and she had seen Nathan vanish up the stairs with Ebony in his arms. That made Scarlett smile. Ebony deserved more happiness then either Ivory or herself could offer. Finding their sister had been their goal since they had realised she was still alive. Only they had wanted to let her settle in with them before they decided to confront the warlock that boasted to be their sire.

The idea that someone so evil was their father made Scarlett feel sick. They had been brought up to appreciate all life, all races. Their mother, from what they'd been told, had always fought for peace. Tried to bring the immortals together in the hopes truces and allies could be made. Only Gregori happened. Their father craved power like Ivory craved ice cream. He wanted it all and he would do whatever it took to get it—even kidnapping an innocent.

Scarlett looked at the screens in Nathan's office, checking each one for any of the Elite Guard and their new

guest. Her eyes became drawn to one in particular, one that showed a male on a chair, his hands tied behind his back. Scarlett was unable to look away. She felt like she already knew the male, although she had never seen him before in her life. The image on the screen was fuzzy and not clear, but she knew he had brown hair that would shimmer with different tones of gold when the sun hit it. His eyes were also brown and again laced with gold, and his lips, the bottom one slightly larger than the top, she sensed would be soft to the touch.

How she knew this, she didn't know—didn't want to know. He was a warlock, their enemy, and it was because of him that Rema had been taken. Patting the screen, she turned and headed for the other door. This one led into the domain of the guards. It was where they trained, where they kept their weapons, and where they held their prisoners. Stepping slowly down the stairs, she kept her eyes and ears alert for any sign of the guards. She had no viable excuse for being in this area other than she was a Princess and could go wherever she liked. Only that excuse wouldn't work anymore. Both her and Ivory had used that gem a so many times in the past that it had lost its effectiveness.

Walking down the corridor, Scarlett peeked inside each room, learning the layout, until she finally found the one she wanted. Slipping inside, she regarded the male, whose eyes were closed. His hair was as she had imagined and so were his lips. Her heart doubled its beats the closer she got. Her fingers twitched, wanting to run through his hair. Scarlett stopped herself two feet away and frowned. This wasn't her. She didn't react to males like this. She never had, even when those of her own race had thrown themselves at her.

"Who are you?" she snapped out. She knew the male

was awake and aware of her presence. Slowly, he opened his eyes—chocolate brown mixed with gold—and regarded her.

"A messenger," he answered simply, his gaze never leaving her face. His stare unnerved her, made Scarlett feel vulnerable—something she didn't like.

"For who? My father?" she asked but received no answer. Just his continuous, penetrating stare. Scarlett moved, not liking his intense gaze. Instead, she walked behind him, until she was looking at the back of his head, at which she scowled.

"What's the message?" she asked, and this time she got an answer. His words seemed deeper, richer in tone, and flowed over her nerve endings.

"Your father wants to meet you—you and your sisters."

"Why?" Scarlett snapped. "He was happy to use our mother and hasn't bothered with us at all. Why should we want to meet him?" Scarlett stopped herself from continuing her tirade. Warlocks were tricksters, only caring about themselves or the power they could gain. She didn't trust any of them. Indeed, if she'd had her way, she would be a pure nightwalker and not the hybrid she was. She felt tainted, unclean—to play host to the warlock blood running through her veins. Especially being the daughter of a monster.

Scarlett had heard the stories of what he had done to those that didn't agree with him. She had made it her task to learn their enemy, knowing, due to her gift, that they would one day have to meet him.

"He didn't give me his reasons, Princess," the warlock answered, yet so far, his answers had not been answers at all. They didn't tell her anything, and that annoyed her. Walking back around to face him, she stopped as his gaze once again pinned her with their intensity.

"That's bullshit. He wants to meet his daughters for a reason and it sure as hell isn't for tea and cakes. Tell me what you know, and I may consider letting you go—or at least not allowing Bishop to beat the crap out of you again." She smirked and folded her arms.

"What I want. Princess, you cannot give me." His voice made her shiver. Usually when someone called her *Princess,* she hated it, but the way this male let it slide off his tongue caused her insides to liquefy.

"Try me, warlock." Scarlett aimed for the cocky and confident approach, not wanting him to know just how much he affected her.

"For starters, *Scarlett,*" as he purred her name, her skin broke out in goosebumps and the hairs on the back of her neck stood straight, "my name is Justin."

The name repeated itself in her head, and the more it was said, the more she liked it. She didn't want to like it, but she did.

"I want a way out," he stated simply. Scarlett tilted her head slightly and regarded the male.

"You want a way out of where, exactly?"

"Gregori's court." His answer this time surprised her, and Scarlett didn't hide that fact.

"If you want out, why have you seen to it that an innocent was taken, why have you assisted him in every way?" Her own voice grew higher in pitch the angrier she got.

"You haven't lifted a finger to stop him and his demented ways. Why the hell should I help you?" Without realising it, Scarlett had stepped closer and, in turn, was now fully aware of Justin's addictive scent. She reacted instantly—instinctually—wanting nothing more than to curl up in the cocoon his arms could offer.

"What the fuck are you doing to me?" she snapped, and

stepped back, hiding the blush of her cheeks in the fall her hair around her face. "You need to cut it out or else I will fetch one of the elite and order them to beat you until you stop," Scarlett threatened despite having no intention of letting anyone beat him. To her dismay, the idea of any harm coming to him made her feel sick to the stomach.

"I am not *doing* anything to you, Princess. My hands and fingers are bound, and as you and your precious elite are aware, my power stems from there." Justin sighed deeply. "With regards your accusations, I had little choice but to do his bidding. Up until recently, that is. Now I want out—and I wouldn't mind seeing him suffer, too. Your *innocent* was a way to get you to him. An excuse."

Scarlett wanted to know more about the reason he had turned and seemed keen to see his lord's demise, but the pain that had briefly flickered across his features told her this wasn't the time nor the place.

Justin continued, "Gregori has no idea about any of you. Your guards have done an excellent job of hiding you from him. So, if I was to return with news that you will meet with him and that you have no powers whatsoever, he will think he has the upper hand..."

"Only he won't," Scarlett finished. She started to pace, a plan already forming in her mind. It could work. As long as both Ivory and Ebony were ready. Their powers as three were still unknown, but they had little time to test any theories.

"How can I trust you?" Scarlett asked, moving closer until she stood only a few feet in front of the male. "You could easily be trying to lure us into a trap set by your lord." Even seated and subdued he was a powerful-looking male. Unlike the warlocks she had seen at council meetings in the past, he was no skinny magic user. No, Justin was tall and

broad. His chest and arms spoke of power—and not of the magic side. Her eyes wandered across his form, taking in every detail. Committing them to memory.

"You have my word. My words are true." He spoke quietly, yet Scarlett felt the truth of his words. She was desperate to believe him.

Scarlett felt conflicted. Did she release him and risk him escaping, or should she trust him and let him help them defeat their father? She closed her eyes and searched for that spark of light deep within. It had appeared the day Ebony had come back into their lives. It felt like an extension of herself and needed little encouragement to come to the surface.

Taking the power, she thought about what she needed, and it responded. It flowed from her in a shower of light, engulfing both Justin and herself in its glow before it receded seconds later.

Only now, Justin was free. Hands no longer bound, body no longer tied to the chair, he stood and moved until he was in front of her. Scarlett flinched as he lifted his hand. She expected a punch, or slap—anything but the feel of his palm gently caressing her cheek. And then he went a step further and shocked the shit out of her.

He kissed her.

SILENTLY, Ebony slipped from her bedroom with her trainers in her hand. Closing the door, she winced as the click echoed in the empty hallway. After what had to have been the most amazing experience of her entire life, she had sneaked out of bed, leaving a snoring Nathan spread-eagled on her bed. The sight would be one she would store away— all that muscle and strength laid out before her... Oh, how she had enjoyed it. Ebony planned to enjoy it a lot more, but she had woken feeling irritable, like there was somewhere she had to be. Strange that the place her gut wanted her to go to was, in fact, the library.

Ebony slipped her trainers on, tucking the laces into the side of the shoe just so her clumsy self wouldn't go tripping down the stairs. As she stood, she watched as Ivory left her own room just as Ebony had left hers. Their eyes met and they both giggled quietly, before they quickly made it down the stairs and headed for the library.

"How's Nathan?" Ivory asked and was rewarded with a blush from Ebony.

"How's Bishop," Ebony countered.

"Passed out and exhausted—just how I like my night-walkers." She laughed and winked. Ivory pushed open the wooden door of the library and they entered the room. Ebony was surprised to see not just Scarlett, but an unknown male as well.

"Scar... you alright?" Ivory asked, a frowned replacing her smile of moments ago.

"Yes, I'm fine. This is Justin. He will be taking us to our father—to get Rema back," Scarlett answered sharply. She stood with her arms folded and a glare plastered on her face.

"And Justin is...?" Ivory asked as she perched on the arm of one of the sofas. Her own gaze not glued on her sister, but on the male in question.

"An ally," Justin responded, and nodded his head. "One that you will need if you want your friend back."

Ebony looked first to Scarlett and then to Ivory, not at all liking the tension that had filled the room. His face was kind, but that meant nothing these days. A blackened soul could be easily hidden behind a good-looking façade. Ebony had learned this early on in life—each foster family she had been sent to seemed perfect on the outside, yet once she was in their house, it quickly changed.

"Really?" Ivory asked sarcastically, then turned her head to look at Scarlett.

"Scar, who is he?"

"Ivory, Ebony, we have to trust him. We don't really have much choice, do we? How else are we supposed to get Rema back? He's the only hope we have right now."

Scarlett rounded the sofa stand in front of Ivory and held her hand out to Ebony. Ebony took it immediately and stood shoulder to shoulder with her new sisters. It was hard to believe that just over twenty-four hours ago she'd been

alone and now she had a family, one that actually wanted her in their lives.

And as she looked from one face to the other, faces so similar to own, she knew, after all the years of living day by day, never fitting in anywhere, she had finally found where she belonged. These two women, who she knew nothing about, had welcomed her, even searched for her. Ebony now had a purpose in life, she had a reason.

She had two sisters, and after what had just occurred upstairs, could now say she had a lover too. One that was protective, overbearing, and downright gorgeous.

Ebony squeezed Scarlett's hand and smiled her support. "I haven't a clue what we're getting ourselves into. I don't even know if I'm going to be any help, but you are my family —Rema is family—and if there's one thing I've learnt in the short time I've been here with you it's that we don't give up on family. You guys cemented that for me when you found me."

Tears filled Ebony's eyes as she spoke. Emotions she hadn't let take control now surged to the forefront. It was amazing how knowing you had somebody in your life that had your back, eased the pressure of living, It was something she would cherish.

"Damn right we're family." Ivory giggled as they all stood smiling at each other. As if rehearsed hundreds of times before, they bent their heads until all three brows touched.

"Family," they said in unison, before all three faced Justin, who was still in the corner of the room.

"Okay, you take us to our father, but I swear if you ever double-cross us, there will never be a place you can hide from us. Understand?"

Scarlett's voice was loud, clear, and serious. The tone alone spoke volumes and showed she would not take any

shit from anyone, least of all this male who had been captured by the Elite Guard.

"Who is he, Scar?" Ivory asked curiously.

"You know the male the guard captured after Rema was taken?" Both Ebony and Ivory nodded, and Scarlett continued, her words now rushing out,

"Well, he is that male and is also a warlock." Ebony watched as a blush stained Scarlett's cheeks, as she looked at the male but hid her face in the fall of her red hair.

"What!" Ebony glared at the male. "You are the reason Rema was taken? What kind of arsehole *are* you?"

Ebony watched Justin wince as she shouted at him. She didn't care. He was the reason an innocent woman had been taken against her will. Ebony knew nothing about their father and the warlocks he commanded, of what they were capable of. However, she was certain of one thing: she didn't bloody trust any of them.

"Whatever. So, what's the plan?" Ivory asked as she left her perch on sofa. "Because if you want to do something, we have to do it quick before both Nathan and Bishop wake up from their pleasure-induced comas." Ivory grinned and wiggled her eyebrows at Ebony.

"I already have a plan," Scarlett answered with a grin. "Ebony, have you still got that journal?" she asked as she walked to the door.

"Yes, of course," Ebony responded, walking over to the chair she'd been perched in earlier and pulling it from under the cushion. She drew it to her chest and followed Scarlett to the door. Ivory and Justin close behind.

"Bring it. We're going to need all the help we can get. First task..." Scarlett said with a grin, "We need to borrow a car."

Sneaking out of the library, they headed for the kitchen

and, in turn, for the back door that lead to the garage. As they all piled through the door, Ebony was stunned into silence at the quantity and expense of the cars that sat in the large space. Walking over to a dark blue Chrysler 300C, Scarlett grinned as she wiggled her fingers and the doors unlocked. Ebony couldn't help but grin back.

"Whose car is this?" Ebony asked as they slid into the plush leather seats. The interior was high-end—no doubt the whole car would have cost more than what Ebony would have made if she had worked in that dingy bar for another three years. There was something familiar about the car that she couldn't quite put her finger on.

"Why it's Nathan's car," Ivory answered innocently as Scarlett started the engine with just a press of a button. She then pulled out a key fob and pressed the button that would raise the garage door.

"Don't worry, though, he won't mind... Maybe," Scarlett continued, and Ebony sunk down into the back seat. That was why the car had been so familiar—his unique scent saturated the interior, and from the look on Justin's face, he wasn't enjoying it half as much as Ebony was.

As the car pulled out of the garage and onto the short driveway, Ebony again wondered what the hell she'd got herself into. Only time would tell if she had the strength to help her sisters and get Rema back. Picking up the worn journal, she started to read, determined to learn what she could.

19

CONSCIOUSNESS RETURNED SLOWLY TO NATHAN. His sleep had been one of the deepest he'd had in a long time. Instead of dreams that were imbued with violence, this time they were filled with visions of Ebony—his Ebony.

He felt lethargic and happy knowing what they had done had been consensual, that she felt the same way he did. Memories of his lips on hers, tasting and learning every curve of her body brought his own to life. Reaching an arm out to pull her warmth into his own, he was met with fresh air and cold sheets.

Sitting up, he looked at the empty space on the bed, slid his hand across the indent identifying where she had been. The cotton was stone cold. Meaning she had been gone awhile and that Nathan slept for longer and deeper than he should have.

"Ebony," he called out, hoping she was in the bathroom. Sliding out from under the duvet, he padded over to the bathroom, not bothering with any clothes. The door was already open, and no one was inside.

His Ebony was gone.

At first, his protective instincts kicked in. He wanted—needed—her back in his arms. But he also knew she had not been brought up to his ways so wouldn't understand the instincts that drove him. Annoyance filtered in slowly, the fact that she had left him asleep grated on his nerves. She had taken advantage of him for some reason or another.

Collecting his jeans, he slid them on and up over his hips. He grabbed his t-shirt and moved towards the door, only to find Bishop on the other side, his fist raised ready to knock.

"Yours gone, too, then?" Bishop asked, running a hand through his hair. He, too, was shirtless and barefoot, a sure sign he'd been left in the same situation Nathan had—high and dry with his female nowhere in sight.

"Yes," Nathan stated simply. "Why, do you have a feeling they orchestrated this together?"

"Knowing Ivory... Yes, they are up to something," Bishop growled out. "Whatever it is, this will be the last time Ivory pulls this shit on me."

"I'm sorry, my friend. I'm starting to get a hint of what you've been through," Nathan admitted as the moved into the hall, heading for the staircase.

"A hint! Nathan, get away now while you still can. These Royals are nothing but trouble," Bishop growled from behind him. He seemed to do that a lot these days.

"I wish I could." Nathan's voice was a mixture of regret and acceptance.

"Shit! She's your mate, isn't she?" Bishop stopped at the top of the stairs, his hand on Nathan's shoulder.

"Yes, Ebony is my mate, the one I've waited centuries for." Nathan smiled at his friend. "And now the only female that has ever managed to run away from me."

"We will find them. It's deciding what we do with them

when we have them that's in question." Bishop grinned as they moved down the stairs and into the hall, heading first for Nathan's office. The house seemed quiet, especially without Rema. A pang of guilt hit Nathan in the chest. He was talking about his mate, celebrating the fact he had found her, when his sister was in the hands of Gregori.

On entering his office, his eyes scanned the network of computer screens across the wall, checking for any sign of the girls.

"Shit!!" Nathan spat as is eyes focused on one screen in particular. "Where's the fucking warlock?"

"Oh, no they fucking didn't!" Bishop ground out. Nathan's heart sank. He knew the girls, especially Ivory and Scarlett, missed Rema. He knew they were confused about who their father was. If this warlock had got to any of them, he could have persuaded them to let him go, and go with him to meet Gregori. He expected as much from Ivory and Scarlett, but knowing Ebony had no doubt gone with them thinking she was doing the right thing twisted his insides and had him wanting to destroy everything in his office. The thought of Ebony going up against Gregori when none of the girls knew what they were doing or had any way to defend themselves made his stomach churn, bile rising in his throat.

"What the hell were they thinking?" Nathan shouted as he turned and walked past his desk towards the cupboard at the back of the room. Opening its doors, he was faced with his own collection of weapons. Pulling on a shirt first, and then arming himself, he pivoted and looked at Bishop. Their bright blue gazes met, understanding reflecting in them.

"Get what you need, Bishop. We're going after them," Nathan stated, Brucking no argument. "We *will* get our mates back."

"You want the rest of the guard?" Bishop asked as he made for the door that led down to the armoury.

"Yes, have them all on standby, tell them to be ready and close by should we need them. The plan is to go in, get the girls, get Rema, and then get out," Nathan ordered, sliding on the leather jacket which hid a now full holster from view. Multiple knives covered Nathan's torso, along with a gun under each arm.

"Why don't we just go after Gregori?" Bishop asked, his hand on the doorknob.

"They are warlocks, Bishop; they have power that we can't beat. What can a nightwalker do against such magic?"

"There is a way to beat them, Nathan—we take their fucking heads." Bishop grinned and then moved out of sight. Bishop didn't need many weapons, he preferred to fight hand-to-hand and would quite happily remove a head with those meaty paws of his.

Nathan looked once again at the screens that covered the wall, hoping he would see one of the girls moving around the mansion. Knowing that if his gut instinct was right, then the possibility of him not making it through the night was high. He wasn't scared—not for himself—but he was petrified for Ebony. She had only been in his world for just over twenty-four hours. This was not the introduction he wanted for her.

Pulling his car keys from his pocket, he looked at the screen that showed the garage and blinked.

"What the fuck!" he shouted as he realised they had not only escaped from the mansion, but they had done it in his brand-new car.

20

Ebony watched as the scenery flew by. Gone was the city lights and bustle of London. Instead, trees and greenery assaulted her eyes, reminding her of the tiny town she grew up in. Memories of being driven by multiple foster parents to and from London just because they couldn't handle her *health issues*.

No one had wanted her, no one had wanted the hassle, and that had hurt, but she could forgive them now. Because without them treating her that way and pushing her to leave, she would have never found her way to the bar, never been in the right place at the right time for her sisters to find her.

This life was nothing she could have ever imagined, not in her wildest dreams, but she embraced it. Just like she would embrace the power her mother's book told her they all held within them. Only Ebony had no idea what it was or how she could access it. She worried that she would only be a hindrance to her sisters and therefore not any help.

Ebony closed her eyes and tried to concentrate, focusing

within herself. The light she had seen before glowed, but then fizzled out like a defective firework.

"You are overthinking everything, Ebony." Justin's deep voice pulled her from her inner thoughts. He had sat in the back of the Chrysler and wasn't happy about it, but Ivory had been adamant that she got 'shot gun'.

"I don't know what you're talking about," she answered, and shot him a glare. She didn't know how he had got Scarlett to free him—he could have put her under a spell for all she knew. She didn't trust him.

"You are trying to force your power to manifest. I can sense it." He sighed, but his gaze kept flicking in Scarlett's direction. Her red-headed sister had done her upmost to ignore the warlock ever since they had set off.

Ebony watched him closely, trying to learn all she could, but she wasn't exactly the best judge of character. His eyes met hers and he smiled. This time, though, it held a hint of sadness—or was it regret?

"Why are you helping us?" Ebony asked. "How can we be sure you won't just fuck us over?"

"I agree," Ivory chimed, turning in her seat to eyeball Justin. "What she said."

"Guys, leave him alone!" Scarlett's hard voice had both Ebony and Ivory turning to look at their sister.

"What the hell has he done to you?" Ivory started, only to turn and glare at the warlock. "What the fuck have you done to my sister? If you've put a spell on her I swear we will pull this car over and I will—"

"You will what?" Justin cut in, stopping Ivory mid tirade. "You will do what exactly? You do realise that my life is forfeit, right? That because I am helping you, there is an almost one hundred percent chance that Gregori will kill me as soon as he sees me."

"Bullshit," Ebony blurted out, feeling her confidence shoot up at knowing she now had at least two people who would back her up. So instead of holding her tongue or whispering under her breath like she had always done, she spoke up.

"He could have quite easily sent you to get capture Rema and then, in turn, get yourself captured to get to us and, as such, lure us out."

"Again," Ivory chirped, "What she said." She grinned and winked at Ebony. "I fucking knew I would like you."

"I should bloody hope so, we *are* related," Ebony countered. Only the whispered answer of the warlock interrupted them.

"I could never or would never hurt you, any of you. Not now". His head had dropped so his chin touched his chest and his hands clenched together. It was almost as if he was dealing with some sort of inner turmoil.

"And why should we believe you?" Ivory asked, only to have Scarlett shout from the front.

"Don't you fucking dare!"

When the warlock lifted his head, his eyes were once again sad, but writhing in their depths was a determination Ebony had only ever seen in the mirror. On those days where she could have easily given in and just fade away. She saw that now as he looked at Scarlett's reflection in the rear-view mirror.

"It's simple," he started. "I could never intentionally hurt my mate or her siblings." With that said, he grinned, shrugged, and turned to stare out of the window. "Take the next left, mate."

Ebony and Ivory both sat stunned. They looked at Scarlett, and then Justin. It was Ivory who spoke first.

"Well, fuck a duck. I didn't see that coming."

S ilence had filled the car for the rest of the journey, and tension thickened the atmosphere. Ebony was certain Scarlett was about to produce smoke from her nose with the way it was flaring, and her grip on the steering wheel had her worrying for the car. In her frame of mind and from the worried glances Ivory kept throwing her way, she wouldn't put it past her sister to wreck the vehicle just to hurt the warlock.

"Are we there yet?" Ivory whispered innocently, which only gained a glare from Scarlett, although it made Ebony snort. Considering the situation, that kind of question just made her want to giggle.

"Nearly, another five hundred yards" Justin answered, and moved in his seat. Worry now etched his brow.

"Why can't we see anything?" Ivory asked. "And is it really wise that we just roll up to the front door?"

"We're warlocks, sweetheart—we tend to glamour where we live," he answered again. "Pull over here, Scarlett." No sooner had she slowed the car down than he was out and walking around to the driver's side. As soon as the car had stopped completely, he had the driver's door open.

"Hey! What the fuck?" Ebony heard Scarlett call out as she was tugged from the driver's seat. She would have been stuck, but Ivory being the smartarse had already unclicked the seat belt.

"Ivory, what the hell are you doing?" Ebony asked.

"Helping my sister get out of her own way," Ivory answered. "Don't get out of the car yet. Let them have their moment."

"But I thought you didn't like him? He's a warlock, isn't

he? Ugh! I'm so fucking confused," Ebony moaned, and closed her eyes. "I thought you didn't trust him."

"I do now," she admitted, before she turned in her seat and knelt on it, giving Ebony her full attention. Although Ebony could see she was itching to see and hear what was happening outside.

"You are new to our world, but let me explain," she started.

"No need to be so condescending." Ebony pouted, only to have Ivory hiss, "Don't be a brat. You need to know these things."

Her playful frown turned into a focused and determined gaze as she continued, "Okay, in our world, when a guy says *mate,* just like Justin did, well... that's serious shit right there. The immortal races don't rely on pathetic things like marriage as the humans do. We have something better—a bond, one that lasts through time. When Justin told us Scarlett is his mate, it means he would rather die than see anything happen to her. Even making her cry would cause him pain. Usually, a mated pair are of the same race, but it would seem it's different for us three, as we're hybrids. We now know we can mate out of the nightwalker race." Ivory grinned and flicked her gaze outside, seeing Scarlett push Justin away and storm off a few metres from the car.

"So as much as I didn't like or trust him as soon as he said he was her mate, the fact Scarlett is throwing one major paddy about it... we know he can be trusted. He may have started off trying to screw us over, but his plan has now changed," Ivory finished. "Get all that?"

Ebony nodded. "Yeah—mate; good; won't hurt us... Got it."

Ivory rolled her eyes. "Come on, let's go break the happy couple up."

"She does *not* look happy."

"She never is. Come on." Ivory slid from the car and slammed the door shut.

Ebony slowly got out, closed the door behind her, and then walked over to where Scarlett was poking Justin in the chest—hard. Her voice was breathless and very, very angry.

"Touch me again, warlock... In fact, breathe near me, and I will cut your balls off and make you eat them."

"She did that once," Ivory commented. "It was real messy." She shrugged as if watching a man's balls being cut off and then eaten was normal. Perhaps for her sisters it was, but for Ebony it was one of the strangest things she had heard that day, and that was saying something.

"Fine," Ebony heard Justin growl to Scarlett, only his gaze said differently. He turned and spoke to all of them. "Your powers, ladies—you are going to need them, and I don't mean the pathetic shit you have as nightwalkers. Being part warlock means you have more power than you could ever imagine and being a blood relative of Gregori means you are so much stronger than you look. One: try and access what you have, if you have any chance of staying alive, you'll need it, and two: don't let Gregori know that you know you are powerful. He thinks you are dumb. Play on that."

"Anything else, Yoda?" Scarlett sneered, her blue eyes sparkling with fury.

"Yes actually," Justin started, "You get yourself hurt, Scarlett, and I may just tie you up, bend you over, and spank you." With each word he stepped forward, until he was face to face with the red-head. Ebony felt herself blush at the words, only to see Scarlett blushing too. She may not like the idea of having a mate who was a warlock, but she wasn't as immune to him as she thought.

"Oooh, he's kinky. You can keep him, Scar." Ivory laughed, earning a single-figured salute in response.

"Err, I don't know about you, but I would rather get this over with," Ebony interrupted as she wrapped her arms around her waist. To say she was scared would be classed as a complete understatement. She was petrified. She had no idea what to expect and no idea how she would deal with the whole father thing—hell, she was so unprepared for this entire lifestyle she was now convinced she was going to die.

"Oh, my god, I'm going to die, aren't I?" she whispered.

"Ebony." She heard her name being called, but the panic attack had started.

"Ebony," a voice shouted, and she felt hands cup her shoulders. "Shh, it's ok. Breathe, sweetheart, we've got you."

Ebony closed her eyes and tried her best to focus on her breathing—a deep one in, then release and repeat. She didn't stop until the sound of her own heart beating in her head had retreated, leaving her with the ability to think a little clearer.

Two sets of blue eyes looked down at her, concern and worry etched across them. The warlock stood a few metres away, pacing, his face directed away from them and down the road.

"Ladies, I suggest you wrap this up." He stood to his full height. "We have company." He turned and faced the road where Ebony could hear tires on the road. This was it.

"I don't know if I can do this," she admitted to her sisters, letting all the fear she felt show on her face.

"You can," they answered.

"How do you know?"

"Because you have us with you. You are not alone."

NATHAN GRIPPED the steering wheel of the Range Rover so hard his knuckles had turned white and there was a danger her would break it. His mind, ever since they had left the mansion, had continuously turned over with the outcomes for all of them.

Most of all Ebony.

"Take it easy on the wheel," Bishop's voice called out, breaking his cycle of thoughts and turning his attention back to his friend. "This baby ain't cheap."

"Only you would have a Range Rover, Bishop. What kind of immortal are you?"

"The practical kind, so be fucking careful with her," Bishop growled as he gripped the strap above the door. Nathan had been surprised that Bishop had thrown him the keys when they had gone to the garage. But when they had slid inside, he had noticed how on edge his friend truly was. He had known Bishop a long time, and he still didn't know his full history. He only knew he was a hybrid, like the girls, only his other half was a damn sight scarier than most realised.

Bishop worked hard to keep that side of himself under wraps, but as Nathan glanced at him, at his hand clenching around the strap hanging from the roof of the car, he saw the strain around his eyes and the tight grip of his free fist.

"You doing okay there, buddy?" he asked quietly, and when he looked again, Bishop's normal bright blue eyes now looked more turquoise.

"No, but there's fuck all we can do at the moment but get to them and get to them quick." His voice was hard, its tone now held a husky edge that vibrated the energy in the air.

"You need to promise me something, Nathan."

"What's that?" Nathan asked, his eyes on the road, the tracking chip that had been placed on the Chrysler doing its job and showing them exactly where they needed to go.

"Once we have the girls, if you can't control me..." He paused. "If I've gone rogue, you either leave me to the warlocks or you kill me yourself." His words had Nathan flicking his gaze to his friend, shock, he was sure, etched across his face.

"No! I will not leave you behind," Nathan shouted. "We don't do that shit. You know that better than most."

"I can't risk hurting her, Nathan. I don't know if my other side even sees her as mine."

The hurt and worry in Bishop's voice struck something deep inside Nathan, but he refused to give up on his friend.

"I won't leave you behind and you won't go rogue," Nathan said with determination.

"Now, what's the plan?"

"Fucked if I know—you're the boss." Bishop laughed, although it was strained. The change of subject had helped to lighten the mood, but only slightly.

"Fuck, great guards we are," Nathan grumbled as the

beep from the tracker sped up, signalling that they were getting nearer.

"Yeah... we are the best," Bishop grumbled. "I've been thinking..."

"Fucking hell—be careful." Nathan grinned and paused for few seconds before he continued, "Go ahead."

"About the guard," Bishop started. "We need to do something to equal the odds with the other races. We are falling behind," Bishop admitted, and Nathan nodded his head. He been thinking the same for a while now, but every time he approached the council, they ignored any sort of request.

"You know the council's views. I was barely able to get permission for the handguns—not that they will help against magic," Nathan grated out.

"That's where we are going wrong, Nathan. Once the girls are back—and now they have Ebony—they have more right to rule over the nightwalkers than those arseholes ever did. Let them rule." Bishop's words penetrated and stuck. If they got out of this situation alive, then he would do just that. The race depended on the council's guidance for survival, only they were merely existing, many falling prey to the other immortal races. Maybe with the girls at the helm, leading, things might get better.

"I think you're right: something needs to change," Nathan started, but growled as he saw his abandoned Chrysler at the side of the road, the doors still wide open and the engine running.

"Let's first see if we can make it out of this alive and with our mates," Nathan said as his eyes scanned for any sign of the girls. As he stopped the Range Rover and slid out, only silence greeted him.

"There's a glamour close. I can feel the energy coming off it," Bishop stated as he walked around the car, his only

weapon of choice in his meaty hand. Nathan eyed it curiously before he started to follow the tracks left behind.

"What happened to the knives?" he called out behind him.

"Nathan," Bishop growled out, "my mate has been taken by warlocks, ones which could quite easily hang me by my balls. My only chance at present is to take their heads, so this little gem... is to the get the job done—properly." He grinned, only this grin showed his bloodthirsty side as he wielded the large double-headed axe.

Nathan nodded again as he followed the tracks. "Come on, they can't be far away now. How close are the team?"

"About five minutes away—and they have the imp, too. He wanted in on any action," Bishop answered before they both fell into silence. Their boots crunched on the dirt road. One moment there was grass and trees, the next they felt like they had stepped through a gateway into another world. The mansion that sat in front of them looked like it belonged in a horror film. The front was littered with old cars, their rusted carcases overgrown with weeds.

"Whoa!" Bishop whispered. "Definitely not what I expected."

"What *did* you expect," Nathan asked, not sure what he'd anticipated either—definitely not what he could see now. The building itself seemed ready to fall down—part of it lacked a roof and many of the windows were smashed.

"I dunno. I thought they were higher market, not trying to model themselves on fucking Dracula." Bishop huffed. "That's our job."

Nathan smirked as he looked for any sign of life. Not seeing any, he started forward again. "Bishop, you go right, I will go left. Find the girls and extract them if possible. Get out quick. Got it?"

Nathan watched as Bishop saluted before he jogged off in his commanded direction, skirting around where the old stables would have been.

Nathan moved off quickly to the left, his gut churning with a sense of foreboding—one that sent shivers up his spine and goosebumps over his arms. A sense that everything he knew would end this night. And his life, if he survived, would never be the same again.

22

EBONY DIDN'T LIKE the mansion—didn't like its run-down, depressing feel. The very walls themselves looked as if they were about to fall down, only the ivy and other foliage holding them together. The inside wasn't much better, the coldness exuding from what felt like every surface, chilled her to the bone, making her shiver as they were led down a corridor. Justin, along with another warlock, led the way.

"You okay?" Scarlett whispered from behind, her body so close Ebony could feel the heat.

"Not really, but hey-ho, what can I do?" Ebony snapped over her shoulder. She was cold and scared.

"Ebony," Ivory whined from behind.

"No, Ivory. I'm cold, this place freaks me out, and I don't know what the fuck I'm doing. You guys have been..." Ebony waved her hands at her sisters, signalling their whole bodies, "you have been *you* your whole lives. You're comfort-able with going head-to-head with a guy that thinks he's a god and who claims he's our father." Ebony had turned around and was now ranting, although she managed to keep her voice quiet.

"I have been Ebony—aka nightwalker, aka warlock—less than forty-eight hours. I've only just learnt I needed to feed, only just fed and then humped the leader of your guard, and now you are expecting me to what...? Wave my magic wand and help you with magic," she hissed. "I am not Harry-fucking-Potter!"

"Who's Harry Potter?" Ivory asked innocently but her comment was ignored.

"Ebony," Scarlett started, but was halted by Ebony's hand in the air.

"Don't," Ebony snapped, and turned to catch up with the two warlocks. As she met up with them, she saw a look of understanding in Justin's eyes before he hid it behind an arrogant smirk.

"Have you finished?" the other warlock sneered. "My master will not like that you've kept him waiting."

"Listen... What's your name?" Ivory asked.

"It does not matter."

"Fine. Listen, grumpy... our father hasn't seen us—like, at all. Ever. I think he can wait another five goddamn minutes, don't you?" Ivory argued, only to have the warlock step forward.

"The only reason you are alive is because he allows it."

"You're a doofus," Ivory answered, only to have Scarlett step in front of her.

"Then please lead the way." Scarlett nodded and waited for the warlock to turn and continue walking down the long corridor.

"Ivory, I swear if you don't keep your gob shut I will—"

"You will what? Don't make promises you can't keep, *Scarlett*," Ivory spat, surprising Ebony with her change of tone as she pushed path both sisters to walk at the front.

Nothing more was said as they all moved towards the

end of the corridor. Ebony was thankful. All the portraits that lined the walls gave her the creeps—she felt like they were watching her. The corridor gave way to a set of enormous doors that were wide open, leading to a grand ballroom that, in its prime, would have been luxurious and full of splendour. Now, however, it looked like a badly-staged version of a haunted mansion, only this one included a throne.

Ebony managed brief glimpses of the expansive room—a large, ornate fireplace, the golds, reds, and oranges of the roaring fire providing the only bit of light and warmth; darkness filled the areas the firelight couldn't quite reach, and things moved, shadows danced, making her skin crawl.

As the girls walked into the ballroom, Ebony found her gaze drawn to the throne and the male that dominated it. His demeanour portrayed boredom as he sat—one leg thrown over the other, he didn't look in their direction. Instead he stared into the fire.

He would have been handsome if it wasn't for the sneer that crossed his face, the light from the fire casting his considerable form in partial shadow, making him look intimidating. Once the girls all stood side by side in front of the throne, he graced them with his attention. A part of Ebony—a very tiny one—had been excited to see her father. He was the only parent she had left, yet the look in his eyes extinguished any hope she had that he would welcome them with open arms.

This man didn't wear a mask to hide his true nature. Indeed, he wore it proudly. There was nothing in his eyes that told Ebony he would let them leave alive.

"Ah, the queen's spawns," he spat out as he uncrossed his legs and leaned on the arm of the wooden throne.

"Ah, Daddy dearest," Ivory hissed in response, which

earned her an elbow from Scarlett. His deep chuckle filled the ballroom and, in turn, the flames from the fire rose higher. They called Ebony's gaze to them.

Ebony looked into the flames and became mesmerised. The flames danced, swaying and enticing her until she placed one foot in front of the other and moved towards their heat.

"Ebony?" she heard Scarlett call out, her voice filled with worry. Ebony ignored her. She wanted to be near the flames. She could hear their voices in her head, urging her to go to them, to relish in their warmth. Every muscle in her body pushed her towards the light. The rational part of her brain warned her against it, but she trusted them. For some unknown reason, Ebony trusted those flames, trusted that they would never harm her. When she stood in front of the fire, she reached out, eager to touch, and as her hand drew near, she watched as a flame leapt from the fire and landed in her hand.

The moment it touched her skin, Ebony felt a rush of power enter her body, pulsing through her bloodstream until she could only scream out, before dropping to her knees. As she held her hand close to her chest, she watched as her sisters made to run to her, only to be stopped by the warlocks. Slowly, she reached out to them as darkness swam in her vision, until it took hold and she saw no more.

S carlett screamed as she watched Ebony drop to the floor. Hands gripped her upper arms, stopping her from running to her sister. What had happened, she had no idea, but she felt a deep need to be by her side—as a sister should.

"Ebony!" she called again but saw no movement as she lay prone in front of the fire, the hand she had placed into its depths clutched to her chest. Why had Ebony gone to the flames? Scarlett turned and faced the man that claimed to be her father, the man that had hunted them.

"What the fuck have you done?" she screamed at him, which only earned her a smirk. "You bastard!"

"Yes, I know I can be," he chuckled in response, and stood from his seat on the throne. His steps were slow and deliberate, each footfall thumped against the wood and matched the sound of Scarlett's heart as it thundered in her chest.

"You are all foolish—foolish to think that I would welcome such abominations and call you my daughters. Foolish to think you could come here and defeat me."

As he drew closer, Scarlett saw he bore little resemblance to either her or her sisters, and she was glad. His words only cemented what she had felt when she had first found out her father was the warlock that had tried to drain their mother of her power after they had slept together. Her mother's diary had been filled with the hatred Queen Angelica had felt for this man, but she had never passed that hate on towards the babies she had growing inside of her. They took after her more than him, and Scarlett was grateful.

Turning her head to the side, Scarlett's eyes met with the tearful ones of Ivory, her arms pinned behind her by the warlock called Clifford. She had always been the soft one, along with being the sister with zero filter. Scarlett felt her fear as Gregori approached, but she also felt guilt. It had been her idea to try and take Gregori on. She watched as his hand cupped Ivory's chin, squeezing it hard. Ivory cried out, the sound cutting through Scarlett's heart.

"Leave her alone," Scarlett ground out, and fought the hold Justin had on her arms. Ivory's quiet sobs filled the ballroom as Gregori turned his attention to Scarlett. He looked from one sister to the other, his permanent sneer making his face as sour as his soul.

"You look like her—you all do" he derided. "You probably take after her too—all of you whores, just like your mother." His words slid over Scarlett's nerves and boiled her blood. About to answer, she found her mouth covered by Justin's hand and his whispered voice in her ear.

"Don't fucking say it, Scarlett." His words caused the hairs on the back of her neck to stand up, but it wasn't from fear. "Just stay quiet—please." It was the *please* that caught her off guard, and Scarlett nodded her acquiescence.

Ivory hadn't received the memo.

"Our mother was not a whore," she shouted, and it shocked Scarlett. She had never seen Ivory get irate. Yes, she said the first thing that entered her mind, giving it an immediate exit through her mouth, but she had never been angry.

"You are a spineless, pathetic excuse for a male. No, wait —you are a twatwaffle," she shouted again. Scarlett watched as her sister slammed her foot onto the instep of the warlock holding her. His arms lowered as he cried out in pain.

"You—" Ivory started again, only to be cut off by a hand around her throat—Gregori's hand.

"Silence!" he roared. He shook a now dangling Ivory, who clawed at his hands in an attempt to get him to release her.

"You bitches have been nothing but a thorn in my side since the day that whore gave birth to you," he sneered, and with ease, he launched Ivory into the air. Scarlett screamed

out as she hit one of the crumbling walls, bricks and mortar raining down on her as she slid to the floor.

"You have been a drain on my power, a power none of you deserve, and I will have it back," Gregori shouted, and rounded on her, only to be interrupted by a roar of ferocity. A blur of black raced through the room, slamming into Gregori and taking him through a wall.

There, in the shadows, facing off with their father, Scarlett watched as Bishop turned and looked at the unconscious Ivory. And then his body changed. Morphing slowly, becoming bigger, broader. His eyes changed from their bright blue to a luminescent green.

"Scarlett, we have to move." Justin's whispered words pulled her gaze from Bishop, but instead of listening them, she yanked free of him.

"No! I have to help my sisters," she cried out, but was unsure who to attend to first—Ivory or Ebony?

"Go to Ivory. I will get Ebony," he answered, and she felt a press of lips to her head before he took off towards the fireplace. Scarlett ran hard for where she had seen her sister drop. Yes, they were immortals, but neither her or Ivory were warriors—hell, Ivory cried every time she got a papercut. Sliding to her knees, Scarlett moved pieces of brick and mortar from her sister's back and pulled her hand onto her lap. She stroked the hair away from her face.

"Ivory... wake up for me sis, come on," she urged, and smiled wide with relief when bright blue eyes met her own.

"What bus hit me?" she asked weakly.

"You tit," Scarlett answered. "Can you move? Because you *really* need to."

Ivory nodded and held on to Scarlett's arms as they struggled to their feet. The sounds of battle—if you wanted to call it that—could be heard.

"What's that noise?" Ivory asked, and they both faced the room where she could see Bishop fighting Gregori.

"That would be your berserker going Hulk mode on Dad," Scarlett answered, looking for Justin, only to see him toe to toe with Nathan. Other males filled the room, ones she recognized as the entirety of the Elite Guard, who surprisingly seemed to be holding their own against the warlocks.

"Bishop," Ivory called out. Her gasp turned into a scream of horror as Gregori threw his hands out and Bishop's body contorted and crumpled to the floor.

"No! Bishop!"

They watched, transfixed, as Bishop made to move, only to have an invisible force pick him up and throw him against the wall, his head connecting with the brick. Energy filled the room as Gregori called on his dark powers.

Scarlett felt the pressure against her skull, the pain increasing with each second.

"We need to get to Ebony," she gasped.

"But what about Bishop?" Ivory cried out, tears flowing freely down her cheeks.

"I don't know, sis. I don't know... Now, come on..."

Rema shivered again, the cold stone at her back and beneath her leached all the warmth from her body. She had no idea how long it had been since she had been taken, all she knew was it was only a matter of time before they came for her again.

Gregori had taken great pleasure in hurting her. He enjoyed every scream that had ripped from her throat.

Rema was scared. The idea of death had never sat well

with her—not after watching Angelica die. But now the thought of never seeing her brother or the girls again made her nauseous. She still had things she wanted to do, places she wanted to see. Maybe fall in love.

Now, like Angelica, she would be denied that.

Tears fell from her eyes and she let them. The *weres,* upon caging her, had deliberately cut her. The loss of blood, although she was now healed, meant she needed to feed. That need would start as an ache but would erupt into a pain like nothing she had ever known. She would then become nothing more than an animal, attacking and feeding on anything that came within distance.

Footsteps sounded in the dark corridor beyond her cage. Rema wrapped her arms around her knees and pushed herself harder against the wall, wanting to make herself disappear.

"Here, pretty, pretty," a voice called out, making her skin crawl. One of the guards had taken a liking to her and loved to torment her.

"I know you are here—I can smell you."

Rema closed her eyes as fear and panic built within. Only the sound of her cage unlocking forced them open. The male, a were named Stan, strolled in. He leered down at her as he smacked a wooden baton into his free hand. The slap of wood on flesh made Rema flinch.

"There she is—my pretty, pretty..." He bent so he was eye to eye with her, his baton touching the skin of her ankle before sliding upwards, taking the material of her ripped skirt with it. "Time to play."

His words oozed from his mouth and made vomit erupt into Rema's own one. She tried to push the baton away from her skirt, only to have the were grip her wrist. Running on instinct, she spat the acid-like substance that has gathered

in her mouth, into his face. On her knees, she scrambled to get away.

"Silly bitch," the <u>were</u> spat out, but grabbed her ankle and tugged, sending her face down into the dirt. His weight was instantly on top of her, his hands fumbling with her clothing.

"This will do—us <u>weres</u> like it from behind." He chuckled, and Rema screamed out. All of her fear and pain were laced in the sound.

"Shut the fuck up," he sneered, and grabbed her hair, tugging so hard he pulled some free, making her eyes water. She felt his clammy hand on her skin. His touched revolted her, but she could no longer move.

"Mmm, soft and warm... is that how your cunt is going to feel when I ram my cock into it?"

His words seared across her ear, and Rema closed her eyes, wishing herself anywhere else.

"I believe that is not the right way to woo a lady," a silky voice cut through the dark. Rema turned her head and opened her eyes. Her cheek was pressed into the floor, but she could still see green eyes and blonde hair.

"Fuck off. I'm busy," the <u>were</u> snapped, and ignored the newcomer.

"That would be a *no* from me, and I think the lady said no, too."

The <u>were</u> growled as he got up from pinning Rema face down and turned on the male, only to start convulsing, cries and grunts erupting from his mouth as he crumpled to the floor in a mass of limbs.

Wide-eyed, Rema curled into a ball, not daring to move any more than that as the male approached and knelt by her side. His lips lifted into a smile that sent shivers of a different nature through her.

"Hi there, I'm Gale. Nathan sent me."

Relief course through her and she smiled back. Gale moved his long hair, which caressed her as he bent and collected her curled up form in his arms. With little effort, he stood, and Rema pushed the locks out of his face.

"Thank you." His voice was deep and soothing.

"No, thank you. You... saved me," she stuttered out, and looked down at the twitching form of the **were**.

"What did you do to him?"

Gale grinned as he walked past the **were,** kicking him hard in the ribs as he did, before he moved out of the cage and slammed the door shut with his foot.

"I tasered the bastard," he stated simply. "It's a lot of fun to watch them twitch."

Rema could do little but smile as Gale carried her away from the cage.

23

NATHAN GRIPPED his daggers loosely in each hand as he circled the warlock that had led the girls and his mate to this hellhole. As soon as they had entered the mansion through the kitchens, both Bishop and himself had waited for the rest of the guard to arrive. Nathan wasn't arrogant enough to think that only two nightwalkers could take on a whole house full of warlocks and survive. Never mind a rescue attempt.

He had sent Angus and Gale to find Rema. He hoped she was still alive, but he wouldn't put it past the warlock to have tortured her. On entering the ballroom, Nathan had quickly realised that stopping Bishop from changing was impossible—the sight of Gregori with his hand wrapped around Ivory's neck had sealed the deal. Now, as he faced his own enemy, he wondered how his friend was faring.

"I don't want to fight you, nightwalker," the warlock proclaimed, which made Nathan frown.

"And why should I believe that?" Nathan shouted over the roar of Bishop—a sign that his friend was still alive. A wave of relief swept through him.

"It's complicated, but I'm trying to protect the sisters as well." The warlock held up his hands and stepped back from Ebony, and Nathan dived forward, bringing her into the cradle of his arms. Her unresponsiveness to his touch worried him, and her skin felt too hot. He was unable to touch her, skin on skin, for long.

"What the fuck have you done to her?" he shouted as he shook her, but still... nothing.

"I didn't do anything. She went to the fire and passed out. My name's Justin," the warlock admitted as he bent near. "Scarlett is my mate. I don't care whether I have your blessing or not—she's mine." With that said, he watched as the warlock raced over to where Scarlett and Ivory cowered, fighting his own kind along the way.

Looking down into Ebony's face again, Nathan couldn't deny what he felt for the little hybrid. She had been thrust into his world, and against his will, had taken his heart. That was the way for his kind—a bond straight from the soul that connected one to the other. All it took was a look, or sometimes a touch. For him, it had been a kiss. One that had sealed his fate to hers. Wherever she went, he would follow, no matter the destination. She was his.

Collecting her in his arms, Nathan moved quickly over to her sisters, not liking the worry and fear on their faces. It was his job to protect them, even from their own mistakes.

"You alright?" he shouted, and they nodded, only Ivory's tears told him she wasn't. Her whispered words grabbed his attention.

"Bishop... I think he killed Bishop," she cried between sobs. Nathan laid the unconscious Ebony down next to her sisters and turned. His daggers once again in his hands, he searched for his friend.

"Watch her and stay here," he ordered, his duty as a

warrior telling him—urging him—to find and help his friend.

"Be careful, Nathan," Scarlett called out. "We are so sorry for this."

"I know," he answered, and weighed in to the fray.

Ebony burned, burned from the inside out, yet she was unable to scream. She felt trapped in her own mind, and she wanted out. The voices that had called her to the fire now filled her skull, their chanted words repeated over and over until finally, she understood them.

Fire, fire, a burning flame. Hot as the sun, the beautiful flame. Give me the power to control you.

Over and over the words sang, until that spark of light she had seen earlier erupted into a full firework display. Ebony's eyes snapped open and her body bowed. Her mouth opened in a silent scream.

Power, raw and untapped power ripped through her being. She felt like her very soul had been torn free and then placed back inside her, only differently. Stronger somehow.

Ebony now had an idea of what had to be done.

24

SCARLETT WATCHED as her newest sister seemed to change in front of her, her body glowing almost like the embers of the fire. Heat and energy pulsed from her, and when her eyes opened, bright blue orbs gazed back at her.

"Ebony," Scarlett whispered.

Ebony smiled weakly and moved her arms to push herself up. Scarlett instantly reached out to help.

"Are you ok? What happened?"

"You look like shit," Ivory acknowledged, and crawled until she sat on the other side of Ebony. "I think, ladies, we may have made a big mistake," she said solemnly as the tears started to erupt again.

Scarlett nodded in agreement, only to duck and cover both Ebony and Ivory's heads as a warlock was thrown over them by one of the guard. Grunts and angry words could be heard as a small battle took place. Only, she felt like there was no way it could end well. Not for them and not for the guard. Scarlett felt guilt rip through her very soul. It was as Ivory had said: it been a mistake to think they could come here and kill their father.

Her own eyes filled with tears and emotion clogged any words she wanted to say in her throat. Everything around them slowed down, like time stood still, as Scarlett watched the men she had grown up with, their protectors fall to the magic of the warlocks. She saw the still form of Bishop as he lay crumpled near Gregori, who now stood waiting for Nathan to approach. Scarlett knew he wouldn't win. How could he?

Her eyes, of their own accord, found Justin. He had claimed they were mates, and she had been a fool to think otherwise. Fate gave them all a chance at finding their soul-mate, and she would have been a monumental fool to have denied that chance. Only now she felt she wouldn't get it. His gaze met her own, and she saw reflected there a sadness that pulled at her heart. In one simple look, Scarlett felt Justin—felt his goodbye.

What had she done?

Lastly, Scarlett looked at her sisters. Ivory, whose emotions matched her own—defeat and sorrow. She looked, as Scarlett did, at Bishop. Ivory had fought his claim on her, but now... maybe she realised that he truly had been the male for her.

Her vision wavered as her eyes filled with unshed tears, as they finally once again met with Ebony's, her orbs now reflecting the bright blue of their kind. Scarlett had brought their sister into their lives only to, in short, kill her. This was not what she had planned. Not at all.

Only Ebony's eyes were not filled with tears or sadness. They sparkled with an intensity that scared Scarlett. Anger, heat, and passion were there, and as Ebony slowly stood, Scarlett followed.

"Ebony?" she whispered again, only to have her new sister smile.

"Time to play."

~

E bony had never in her life felt as strong or as powerful as she felt at that very moment. When she had initially been drawn to the fire, she had chastised herself for being a fool. For allowing her weak mind to be bewitched. She had feared for all the people she had come to care about that her weakness would be their downfall.

Only the fire had done the opposite. Whatever Gregori had hoped to achieve by them being there, or by her succumbing to the call of the fire, would not happen. Not now and not whilst she breathed.

She had welcomed the fire and welcomed and accepted that spark deep inside that had been locked away. She had been unable to reach it due to not believing or feeding.

Now though... Oh, now Ebony believed.

The spell that had chanted in her head was now seared behind her eyelids. She would never forget it, nor would she want to, and as she stood, Ebony knew, that although the odds seemed against them—t

hey weren't.

Turning, she looked at the defeated faces of her sisters. Tears stained their dusty cheeks and Ivory still sat in the floor, her forehead oozing blood. Her head was bowed as she sobbed.

"Scarlett... Ivory," Ebony said confidently, and held her hands out to both, She smiled as first Scarlett accepted, then Ivory, who slowly got to her feet.

"You have to listen to me. Ok?" She started, and she met both their gazes, one at a time, determination in her own

that she hoped she could pass onto them. Make them see that all it would take was self-belief.

"This may sounds nuts, but close your eyes for me."

"Ebony, this isn't the time. We are stood in the middle of a bloody war zone," Ivory cried out.

"Just do it, please."

"Fine," Ivory huffed, which she followed with a sniff as she closed her eyes. "We are probably dead anyway, so why not."

Scarlett remained silent but squeezed Ebony's hand as she also closed her eyes. Ebony waited a few seconds.

"Okay, look deep within... deeper than you ever have done before. What do you see?"

"Nothing," Ivory answered.

"Look harder," Ebony whispered.

"What am I looking for? Bloody hell, Ebony, this isn't the time."

"Ivory, shut up and look," Ebony growled out, and Ivory snapped her lips shut. Ebony knew what was going on around them. She knew time was of the essence. But this could be the difference between living and dying.

"I see a light," Scarlett called out, and Ebony squeezed their hands again.

"I do too," Ivory also called out. "What is it?"

"Go to it, trust in it... trust in you," Ebony answered.

Ebony beamed as both of her sisters smiled and sighed, as they both started to glow. Because Ebony had been unused to anything of the magical variety, when she had accepted the power, it had knocked her out. Only Ivory and Scarlett wouldn't be—they had used a small portion of their powers before, so wouldn't be as affected.

A light breeze stirred around them, swirling in the middle of the ballroom. Caressing them. Mist, light and

gentle, fell on her skin as the scent of earth, deep and woody, filtered through her senses.

They were the sisters of prophecy.

Three sisters with the power to control the four elements.

Fire,

Air,

Water,

Earth.

Ebony grinned this time as both sisters' eyes snapped open and met hers.

"Shit," Scarlett whispered.

"Well fuck-a-doodle-doo," Ivory laughed.

"As I said, ladies: it's time to play," Ebony said, and turned. Clasping each other's hands, they gave themselves willingly to the power.

25

Nathan faced Gregori—the male of legend, some would have said. Others said he was a menace to the immortal races. His own quest for godhood had been the cause of many deaths to not only nightwalkers, but to demon, fae, **were**, and others.

His need for power had the councils petrified, and his search for the princesses had been more than just a pain in the arse for Nathan.

Time and time again his guard had protected them from his continuous attempts at kidnapping or murder. He had hoped the girls had been unaware, but after seeing Ivory and Scarlett face Gregori down, he knew that they had been more aware of everything that had gone on than he would have personally wanted.

"So, the famous nightwalker," Gregori sneered. "It's a shame really—that such a prominent annoyance in my life is about to be snuffed out." Gregori sighed.

"Confident in yourself, aren't you," Nathan replied. His seemingly relaxed stance belied his tension, each muscle was bunched ready to move. He wouldn't get a second

chance to take Gregori down, this he knew. The warlock was far too powerful, but that didn't mean he wouldn't try.

"Well, you know I am the king," Gregori answered smugly. His hand reached up, and Nathan prepared himself.

"See that up there?" he said, pointing to the **were** that had been fused to the wall. Now dead, his body hung there, parts rotting. With his full attention on finding Ebony, and then aiding his friend, he'd somehow failed to both see and smell it.

"That's what I do to immortals that annoy me." Gregori paced a little, his arms gesturing. "He was very much alive when I put him up there. You see, he was the **were** that failed to get the pathetic creature that calls herself my daughter. Because you were in the way." Gregori sighed and looked again at the body of the dead immortal.

"He was still alive this morning, thrashing about, trying to get free, ripping his skin and muscle from the wall. All that blood and mess on the floor." He clicked hi tongue.

"Right, because this place is so clean," Nathan interrupted sarcastically. He was happy for the warlock to spend all day talking if it meant it would keep him busy. Giving his men and the girls chance to get away.

"Silence! Don't make me rip out your heart like I did him. His moaning got on my nerves, and frankly, your voice is beginning to as well," the warlock snapped. The way he paced reminded Nathan of a caged animal, the type of beast that would turn on its caretaker.

Instead of answering, Nathan just smirked. He wanted the warlock rattled, but not enough that he would attack. *Keep him busy*, he repeated in his mind.

"You've done well, you know, nightwalker—keeping them alive. Although you nearly dropped the ball with the

dark-haired one," Gregori taunted. Nathan clenched his fists around the hilt of the daggers he had palmed.

"All three of them are weak, but that one really should have died at birth. All of them are mongrels. A cross of breeds that should have never happened," he continued, and Nathan let him despite every bone in his body urging him to take his head.

"Worry not, once they are dead, which will be soon, I will inherit their powers as I should have done when their mother died. Stupid bitch. Getting pregnant just to stop me."

Nathan stepped forward, each word spoken by Gregori increased his blood pressure. His fangs, which had already dropped with adrenaline from the battle, now pierced his lower lip. His steps faltered as the sound of battle faded, leaving only the cracking of the fire and the whisper of gentle footsteps. Nathan turned his head and saw Ebony first, her eyes glowing in the dim light and her hair blowing around her as if caught in a phantom storm. Ivory and Scarlett walked by her side. All three had joined hands.

"Ebony," he called. She should have been trying to get out, not walking up to the warlock like they wanted to chat. Moving quickly, he noticed Gregori twirling his fingers, a fireball starting to build in shape. Pumping his arms, Nathan raced towards the princesses.

"Get down," he shouted, "Get fucking down!" Only his words were ignored, and as he glanced behind him, he watched a grinning Gregori release the ball. The fire shooting its way in a direct line towards his target.

The target being Ebony... His mate.

Throwing himself into its path, he wrapped his arms around Ebony. Covering her smaller form with his own. The impact knocked the breath from Nathan, but he didn't care.

Ebony was alive, but only as he struggled to take another breath did he realise his chance at defeating Gregori had gone. But that had never been his fate.

He had been chosen to protect, yet even now he wouldn't be able to complete the job. His arms still wrapped around Ebony's shoulders, he looked into her eyes. The blue matched his own yet was void of recognition. She still stood hand in hand with her sisters, and energy flowed around them. Releasing his hold, he stumbled back, oxygen getting harder and harder to take in. A burning pain swept through him, sending him to his knees. This was not how he wanted to go out.

The daggers he still gripped slipped to the stone floor as his vision clouded. On his knees, Nathan watched as the sisters slowly walked past him, none giving him a second look.

"Ebony," he whispered once more, before darkness took him, what small breath he had leaving his body as it hit the floor.

Ebony felt like she was watching a movie, one in which she was in a starring role. She was facing death, only she didn't feel scared. Neither did Scarlett or Ivory. Their feelings connected with her own and gave her courage. Only, she had no control over her body as it walked straight towards Gregori.

You guys able to move? Ebony asked in her head, not sure if anyone would hear her, but something told her they would.

Why can I hear you in my head? Ivory chirped. *I don't like listening to myself in my head, what makes you think I want you in here?*

Oh, shut up! Scarlett replied. If Ebony's facial muscles could actually move, she would have smiled.

Anyone able to move—at all, Ebony repeated. She wasn't enjoying not being able to control her body, not when Gregori was now looking at them and swirling his fingers. Ivory was the first to mention it.

"What's he doing?"

"I don't know, but I don't like it," Scarlett replied.

"Is that a fireball?"

"Yes, of course it is. What did you expect him to produce...a snow ball?"

"I don't know. I've never met him before."

"Err, guys... Shouldn't we be moving out of the way? And why can't I control my body!" Ebony almost shouted. Panic surged within, but it only got so far before it was pushed away. She watched as a malicious grin spread across his face before he launched the fiery ball directly at them. Only it wasn't big enough to hit them all—no, this one was aimed at her.

Shit! What do I do, what do I do? she asked, only to see Nathan sprint across the room, his arms pumping. And then he was standing in front of her. His arms wrapped around her shoulders moments before the ball hit.

Nonononono! Ebony cried out as the impact hit Nathan in the back. His body jerked and she saw pain etch across his face.

Nononono... What were you thinking? Nathan... Nononono! she screamed out, desperate to take him in her arms. She heard him whisper her name and saw the pain and sadness when she didn't answer him. Instead, her body and those of her sisters simply stood there.

Nathan back away and Ebony missed his touch immediately. She wished with all her heart that they were back in her room at the mansion, buried under the duvet together. He slid out of view, and Ebony screamed in her head. But her body did its own thing. The power they had claimed now claiming their bodies to do their bidding.

What the hell is going on, how do we get control back? she cried out.

We have to trust in the power, Scarlett answered.

Ebony was about to tell her sister to politely fuck right

off, that yes, she had said before to trust in it herself, but how could she trust something that had taken over her body until she had no control? Because of the power, she had just watched as the male she was starting to have very intense feelings for took a killing blow. The look of pain and hurt in his eyes would remain with her forever. Only, she couldn't dwell on that. Her body, along with her sisters', stopped. Their hands still clasped, they now looked at their father. His pacing form not two metres away didn't look happy.

"That power is mine! You have no idea what you are doing," he spat out.

He may be a twat, but I agree. Ivory's voiced flowed into Ebony's mind. They were all just going with the flow— Gregori was right. They hadn't a clue what to do now. Calling on the power had been the easy part. Controlling it and using it was a whole different matter.

He may be right, but we need to do something... Ebony answered.

As the words whispered though her mind, Ebony felt a shift. The power vibrated through her body until every extremity tingled and she was able to move her fingers.

I can move my fingers, she shouted through their bond, but as feeling returned to her whole body, she felt like she was unable to hold her own weight. The tight clasp and pull on her own hands told her both Ivory and Scarlett were dealing with the same issue.

"See, you have no control." Gregori laughed as all three dropped to their knees. "You are weak and pathetic, just like your nightwalker guard. You will die, and the power will come to me," he shouted confidently. He raised his arms wide. His lips moved, but Ebony couldn't make out the words. Dragging her eyes away from the warlock, she looked to her sisters. Both leaned on their hands, trying to

deal with the energy coursing through them. All Ebony wanted to do was close her eyes and rest. The flow and ebb was becoming too much. She finally gave in and closed the only words, echoing and powerful, filled her mind.

Water, water, blue as the sky. Give me the power to control you with my mind.

Fire, fire, a burning flame. Hot as the sun, the beautiful flame. Give me the power to control you.

Earth, earth, beautiful earth. Give me the power to control you.

Air, air, the invisible, deadly force. Give me the power to control you.

"Can you hear that?" she shouted as she opened her eyes again and looked to the side. Both sisters looked back at her, nodding their heads.

As the spell repeated, growing louder and louder, she felt that answering pull deep down inside her. Deep down where that original spark had been. Forcing herself to her feet, Ebony took a deep breath. Her eyes fell on Nathan, his slumped form breaking her heart. She didn't know if he was alive or not. She looked at Bishop, who she had thought was dead, only he now seemed to be trying to move. The rest of the nightwalker guards—men she had yet to meet—were scattered across the room. Warlocks lay dead or injured around them.

And all for what?

This selfish, arrogant man who craved power, who relished in death and destruction.

As she turned, she again looked to her sisters, and saw them standing too, their gazes filled with uncertainty.

"What do we do?" Ebony asked.

"We say those words," Scarlett answered.

"Which ones? The ones going around and round in my head?" Ivory called.

"Yes!" Ebony and Scarlett replied, hope swelling deep inside.

"Water, water, blue as the sky. Give me the power to control you with my mind," Ivory chanted, her voice rising with every word.

"Fire, fire, a burning flame. Hot as the sun, the beautiful flame. Give me the power to control you," Ebony followed, energy pulsing through, her making her own voice rise to match that of Ivory's.

"Earth, earth, beautiful earth. Give me the power to control you," Scarlett joined in, her own beautiful voice calling out.

Finally, all three chanted in unison as completed the spell.

"Air, air, the invisible, deadly force. Give me the power to control you!"

Like before, the elements swept around them, filling the air and their senses. Ebony reached out a palm, and before her eyes a ball formed, inside a bright red pulsed as it caressed her skin.

Fire.

Scarlett did the same in her own, and a ball filled with greens and browns pulsed before her eyes.

Earth.

Ivory grinned and held her hand out. She squealed as a ball formed in her palm. Inside, a clear fluid rushed from side to side.

Water.

A deep breeze filled the ballroom and swept around them as the fourth element answered their call. Air, too powerful to be contained in a simple ball, whispered across their senses.

"What have you done?" Gregori screamed. "You have no right. It belongs to me!"

Ebony smiled as Scarlett spoke, her voice sounding loud and confident.

"No, it doesn't belong to you. It is ours, as is our destiny." She stepped forward and lifted her free hand. Instantly, the air answered her, sweeping around them in a cyclone—like a shield.

"You will never hurt us," she shouted.

Gregori's eyes bulged with anger and he shot his hands forward. Dark energy blasted from them. It reminded Ebony of an arrow made of dark, black mist, only as soon as it hit Scarlett's barrier, it vanished. Incensed, he created his own fire ball, shooting it once again at Ebony, who sent one of her very own right back. She grinned in delight as his fizzled upon Scarlett's barrier, whilst hers was a direct hit.

Striking him in the chest, she watched as his body was thrown into the curtained wall behind. Brick and mortar came loose, along with the curtain. The rotting velvet gently floated from the wall, revealing a stunningly beautiful mirror. One that stood over ten feet high and five feet across. The glass was aged, tarnished in places. Gregori slowly got to his feet, using the mirror to help him stand. He glared at them.

"You think you have won?" he shouted as he stroked the surface of the mirror. The gleam in his eyes worried Ebony, yet she didn't move. They wanted to remain behind the safety of the barrier.

"You may have stopped me for now, *daughters*," he sneered the word, "but this is just the beginning." Lifting his free hand, he twirled his fingers. All three watched as the surface of the mirror changed, becoming almost liquid-like.

"Shit! He created a portal," Scarlett yelled, and released

her own ball, throwing it at him. Its aim was true, until the warlock, Clifford, appeared to help his master, dragging a severely beaten and unconscious Justin with him. The ball hit, turning the warlock into stone and throwing both him and Justin through the portal.

"No!" Scarlett cried.

The air that had been creating a barrier dissipated as soon as Scarlett's concentration broke. The pain in her voice breaking the spell, they were now left vulnerable. Ebony stepped closer to her sisters as Gregori also noticed the drop in power too, his hand already creating the same fireball Ebony now could. Only he didn't need time or pure effort to do it. His dark arts answered his call immediately.

"Maybe you haven't won after all," he said and moved to throw the ball at them. Ebony closed her eyes, not wanting to see it coming. Ivory screamed out.

"No, Bishop, don't!"

The fallen nightwalker had got to his feet and was now barrelling towards Gregori. A roar left his mouth as the fireball that had been meant for them hit him directly in the chest, but that didn't stop him. In a few steps, he had Gregori around the throat and through the portal. Both vanished from view. Seconds later, the mirror's surface returned to its original state.

Silence filled the ballroom, but only for a few seconds before a scream then filled the room. Ivory raced to the mirror, her fists banging on the surface as she screamed for Bishop.

"No, you bastard. You said you wouldn't leave me...you promised!" she sobbed as she slid to her knees, her body pressed to the glass.

"You said you would never let me go!"

Ebony watched as Scarlett moved towards Ivory, as she

knelt down and took her in her arms. Scarlett's own face showed heartbreak. They had watched Justin vanish too.

There was little doubt Scarlett had some sort of feelings for the warlock, but how intense they were, Ebony didn't want to ask. Her own heart hurt, the pain a pulse that got deeper with every heartbeat. Her own tears fell, sliding down her cheeks as she turned and moved towards Nathan.

His crumpled body, covered in dust, lay still. Slowly, Ebony slid to her knees and reached out to touch his broad back, just under the large wound where Gregori had hit him. The gaping hole was filled with charred flesh and blood.

Memories of their time together filled her mind. His intense blue eyes as they looked at her from above, the feel of his hands on their skin, and the way he shouted, *Mine*. She had felt wanted. He had risked everything for her, and what had she done to say thank you?

She had gone off without telling him, forcing him to follow and now... Now he lay dead because of her. She stroked his back again, memorising the play of each muscle. His warmth seeped through the thin t-shirt he wore.

Warmth?

Ebony gasped. Moving quickly, she looked at the hole in his back before she rolled him onto his side. Placing her hand on his chest, she waited—waited until she felt the slow rise and then fall of his chest.

Nathan was still alive.

NATHAN'S WHOLE BODY ACHED. He couldn't take a deep breath in and his arms and legs refused to answer his bidding. He was dying—he knew that. Hell, as soon as the fireball had hit him he thought he had been a goner instantly. Only he wasn't that lucky.

No, his last moments on this world would be listening to his own breath rattle in his chest. Or so he thought. Sobs filtered through his mind at the same time as he felt a warm touch to his back. His heart pounded, making the pain from his back worsen.

A gasp followed, then small hands pushed his heavy form over and he was able to look up into the beautiful face of his mate. Her blue eyes swam with tears and made dusty tracks down her cheeks.

"Nathan," she whispered as she cupped his cheeks. They felt soft and welcome. Nathan attempted to smile.

"Hey, Princess," he answered despite every breathe causing him intense agony.

"Nathan, what do I do?" Ebony asked him, her voice full of worry. "Tell me," she cried.

"It's ok," he answered as he lifting his hand and cupped her cheek, rubbing his thumb across a tear track. "There's nothing you can do."

"There has to be," she almost shouted. "Aren't you immortal? Surely you can heal or something... Nathan, you can't go."

"Immortal to a point, Princess. Even nightwalkers can't heal from magical fireballs," Nathan coughed out.

"Well that's not fucking good enough," Ebony cried. She leaned over him and touched his lips with her own. The feel of them broke Nathan's heart. He had loved this woman since the day he had seen her.

"You need to go." He coughed again, pain flooding his system. His lungs burned and darkness again swam across his vision.

"No. I won't leave you," she sobbed. He felt her forehead against his own. "I can't leave you, Nathan, not when you own a part of me." Her tears fell in steady streams.

"I love you, mate," Nathan whispered, as he reluctantly gave in to the darkness.

"Nonononononono!" Ebony screamed and threw her head back, pain like nothing she had felt before ripped through her, splitting her heart in two.

"No... No, this is not happening. I will not let this happen," she shouted. Yes, they had made the mistake of coming here, but that didn't mean they would lose everything. Ivory had lost her man, Scarlett had lost the chance at her happily ever after, and now Nathan.

No, fate was not that cruel, and if it was, she would fight it. Ebony felt hands on her shoulders as her sisters knelt next to her. Sobs that weren't her own joined hers as Rema appeared. She scrambled from the arms of a male and flew to Nathan's side. The rest of the team that had somehow survived stood, heads bowed.

The warlock had cost them much. But Ebony wasn't finished.

Taking hold of her sisters' hands, she closed her eyes and searched once again within herself. She didn't need the immense power they had tapped into before. No, she needed her power as a nightwalker. Her sisters had theirs,

now she wanted to access hers. She didn't know if it would work, but she wouldn't give up.

Focussing deep within, she found it, a small ball of colour infused light—purples, blues, and greens. Both sides of herself sat in that one ball of white light, vibrating with so much power Ebony was nervous of it and yet next too it the opposite, one filled with love and hope.

This was her very essence, what made the new Ebony tick. Pulling on it, she smiled as it flowed through her, filling every inch of her being. Rightness filled her soul as she released the grip she had on Ivory and Scarlett and placed her hands on Nathan. His cold form bowed in response as she poured everything that she had into him. Pushing the power, urging him to heal.

Gasps could be heard and Ebony opened her eyes. Nathan was surrounded by colour, his body cocooned within its depths. The power she had released pulsed and vibrated, before it dissipated.

Ebony waited, and what felt like an eternity passed before she saw the clear rise and fall of Nathan's chest. Her hands roamed over him and checked the wound on his back. The charred and shredded flesh was now whole and healed.

"Wow, Ebony," Ivory whispered and wrapped her arms around Ebony's neck. Scarlett's followed suit as they sat there, stunned.

"Wow," Ebony repeated before all three started to giggle. Although the smiles from her sisters didn't meet their eyes. Ebony gripped their hands.

"We will get them back," she said.

"I promise."

"Princess Scarlett, Princess Ivory, Princess Ebony, what a pleasure to finally have you here at council." The arrogant voice of the councillors filled the chamber and made Ebony twitch from her seat. As Royals they had been seated on thrones on a raised plinth at one end of the room. They had been ordered by Rema and Nathan that they were to dress the part, so all three were now dressed in gowns of the finest quality with matching tiaras.

Ebony felt like a twat.

"Take that sour look off your face and smile," Nathan whispered in her ear from his position behind her. Ebony snorted quietly.

"You try wearing a corset and see how you feel," she snapped back, and was rewarded by a gorgeous smile as she turned her head to the side.

His eyes filled with heat, and he smirked as he bent forward again. "I would much rather see you in it—in only that," his voice turned husky, "as I bend you over."

Ebony hissed and moved in her seat as heat flooded through her system.

Her whispered "behave" was rewarded with a chuckle as he returned to his place, and Ebony tried to concentrate on the council meeting and not her mate's promise.

Since the battle at the mansion and Ebony's discovery of her power, things had been different. For her the whole experience was different. She now had a family. Yes, it was a strange one, but she loved them all dearly. Rema had recovered from her own experience, although she wouldn't talk of it. Nathan worried dearly but Ebony had informed him women were a lot more resilient than he gave them credit for.

To say she had accepted Nathan's claim on her was an understatement, and, in turn, Ebony had staked her own claim on the nightwalker and intended to make it official. She knew the council would not like it and she didn't care. The throne belonged to her and her sisters, and no pompous arse was going to force them into doing anything.

They were complete and were now training themselves to wield the power they had. They'd agreed that now was the time to, in short, rule their race. The battle had shown them all, the guard included, that times had changed and the warlocks were more powerful than they had ever given them credit for. The other races would need to band together if they ever had a hope of peace.

Ebony grinned as Scarlett stood and moved down the steps, the skirt of her gown sweeping across the floor. They had appointed her their spokeswoman as she was the only one out of the three of them that took zero crap. Ebony felt nothing but pride as she walked onto the floor to begin her speech.

What was about to be said would change the course of their future and, in turn, the future of other races.

"Councillors, I and my sisters thank you for inviting us

here. Having spoken with the leader of our guard we are aware of your insistency to see us wed and the royal line continue. That being said..."

Ivory giggled and bounced in her seat, which made Ebony laugh. They both knew what was coming and had been excited. Ivory had wanted to bring popcorn, but they had all decided against it. Worried it may show them up as being less than royalty.

Nathan's growl made them sit still as they listened to Scarlett's well-formed words.

"We will *not* be forced into any marriage that is of your saying," Scarlett said with such confidence a few of the councillors bowed their heads.

"It is time, my fellow nightwalkers, that we continue what our mother started—to unite the immortal races and bring peace. I thank you for your loyalty, but it is time for myself, Ivory, and Ebony to rule."

Arguments erupted, only Scarlett held up her hand and silence returned. "In light of this, I am happy to announce that both myself and Ivory have given our blessing to the joining of our sister, Ebony, and the leader of our Elite Guard, Nathanial." Scarlett beamed.

Once again, voices of outrage filled the room and, in turn, the Elite Guard moved forward, putting themselves in front of Ivory and Scarlett, with Nathan stood beside Ebony. Anger could be seen on all the councillors faces, not at all happy of the changes that were occurring, and yet Scarlett smiled.

"Ebony," she called. Ebony stood and took a step forward, aware of her mate right behind her. Holding out her hand, she called silently to the power of fire. A task she had been practising constantly since they had returned.

Instantly, a ball appeared, like it had at the battle, and

she grinned, then looked to her sister, who held up a hand, gesturing.

"See, gentleman, we are no shrinking wallflowers that need a man to lead us." Her sarcastic tone silenced the males. Ebony slowly walked down the steps, along with Ivory, and stood shoulder to shoulder with Scarlett.

"We have claimed the power that was our mothers, your queen's, and now we claim the throne as is our right. Those that dispute our claim know this..." Scarlett held her hand out, as did Ivory, until all three of them stood with their powers showing, as balls of energy filled their palms. Earth, fire, water. The power that was air was present in the breeze that swept through the room. Ready to answer their call when needed.

"We are prepared to fight... Are you?"

The prophecy had begun.

To be continued...

EPILOGUE

THE LEGEND of the Berserker was a short one, steeped in Norse mythology, it spoke of warriors given the power of strength and fury by the gods. Their ability to wage war and yet feel nothing became a sought-after skill. Their trance-like state and bloodlust was frightening, yet beguiling.

To have as Berserker at your side brought with it invincibility. To have one as your prisoner meant you had one at your beck and call—if only you could control the beast. Gregori looked down at the chained form of the nightwalker. He was more than he seemed.

The possible last of his kind. A half breed, yet... he could be what he needed to get back what had been taken from him.

He had an animal at his command, one that would give him what he had failed to get before. What he wanted more than anything:

The princesses' dead.

Ivory's Beserker-Book 2 Trinity series

ABOUT THE AUTHOR

J. Thompson is a USA Today Bestselling Author of Paranormal and Sci-Fi romance and a major fan of procrastination. Jenn has always loved history, so using her wild imagination and tying in her love of history and fantasy, she began a new adventure into the world of words. Weaving romance into old worlds and giving life to her mythical inspired novels is what Jenn does best, and she has a lot more planned in the future, including some hard assed demons.

When she isn't bent over her laptop with the crazy writer eyes, you will find Jenn making jewellery, cross stitching and it doing paper crafts. Jenn is also an avid lover old skool skills like archery and sword fighting.

Maybe a touch nuts Jenn is an author who believes wholeheartedly that people are good and that everyone deserves romance - even Hades.

For regular updates sign up to Jenn's Newsletter HERE

ALSO BY J THOMPSON

Dragon it Out Coming 2022

Co-authored

Dragon fire and Phoenix Ash

Draakon Desire Series

Raanar-

Stand Alones

Exercise in Love

Magic and Mayhem Universe

Witch out of Water-Kracken's Hole Book 1-https://magicandmayhemuniverse.com/j-thompson/

Tail of a witch- Kracken's Hole Book 2-https://magicandmayhemuniverse.com/j-thompson/

Witch out of Luck- Kraken's Hole Book 3-https://magicandmayhemuniverse.com/j-thompson/

Altorian Cyborgs

Betraying Ko'ran

Jorah's Revenge- Coming 2022